PUFFIN BOOKS

Tickled Onions

A generous serve of stories from one of Australia's funniest authors.

Kids in a pickle, parents in a jam – these tales are bursting with the flavour of fun.

Warning – may cause tears of laughter.

Also by Morris Gleitzman

MORRIS GLEITZMAN

Tickled Onions
and other funny stories

PUFFIN BOOKS

Get Reading! is an Australian Government initiative developed through the Australia Council for the Arts.

PUFFIN BOOKS

Published by the Penguin Group
Penguin Group (Australia)
250 Camberwell Road, Camberwell, Victoria 3124, Australia
(a division of Pearson Australia Group Pty Ltd)
Penguin Group (USA) Inc.
375 Hudson Street, New York, New York 10014, USA
Penguin Group (Canada)
90 Eglinton Avenue East, Suite 700, Toronto, Canada ON M4P 2Y3
(a division of Pearson Penguin Canada Inc.)
Penguin Books Ltd
80 Strand, London WC2R 0RL England
Penguin Ireland
25 St Stephen's Green, Dublin 2, Ireland
(a division of Penguin Books Ltd)
Penguin Books India Pvt Ltd
11 Community Centre, Panchsheel Park, New Delhi – 110 017, India
Penguin Group (NZ)
67 Apollo Drive, Rosedale, North Shore 0632, New Zealand
(a division of Pearson New Zealand Ltd)
Penguin Books (South Africa) (Pty) Ltd
24 Sturdee Avenue, Rosebank, Johannesburg 2196, South Africa

Penguin Books Ltd, Registered Offices: 80 Strand, London, WC2R 0RL, England

This collection published by Penguin Group (Australia), 2010
This collection © Creative Input Ltd, 2010

Individual stories copyright © Creative Input Ltd
First published by Penguin Group (Australia)
'Imagine That' first published in *Kids' Night In 3*, 2009
'Odd Socques', 'Paparazzi' and 'Good Dog' first published in *Give Peas A Chance*, 2007
Earlier versions of parts of 'Secret Diary of a Dad' were first published in *Kids' Night In*, 2003, and *Kids' Night In 2*, 2005
'My Problem Is I Don't Know When To Stop' first published in *Wow! 366 Speedy Stories in Just 366 Words*, Scholastic, 2008

10 9 8 7 6 5 4 3 2 1

The moral right of the author has been asserted.

All rights reserved. Without limiting the rights under copyright reserved above, no part of this publication may be reproduced, stored in or introduced into a retrieval system, or transmitted, in any form or by any means (electronic, mechanical, photocopying, recording or otherwise), without the prior written permission of both the copyright owner and the above publisher of this book.

Cover and text design by Cameron Midson © Penguin Group (Australia) 2010
Cover illustration by Greg Rogers
Typeset in 13/18pt Joanna by Post Pre-Press Group, Brisbane, Queensland
Printed and bound in Australia by McPherson's Printing Group, Maryborough, Victoria

National Library of Australia
Cataloguing-in-Publication data:
Gleitzman, Morris, 1953–
Tickled Onions
ISBN 978 0 14 330560 6
I. Title
A823.3

puffin.com.au

Mixed Sources
Product group from well-managed
forests and other controlled sources
www.fsc.org Cert no. SGS-COC-004121
© 1996 Forest Stewardship Council
FSC

For
Ben and Rebecca
Sophie and Jamie

Contents

Draclia

Corey woke up suddenly.

It was dark. At first he wasn't sure where he was. In his ear a squeaky voice was hissing something about blood.

Corey blinked. He could just make out a shadowy figure looming over him, pressing him into the pillow. A figure with big staring eyes and white teeth.

Corey didn't panic.

He waited till he could see better.

Yes, it was just as he'd feared. He was being pinned to the bed by a five-year-old boy in dinosaur pyjamas clutching a blue plastic truck.

'Will,' groaned Corey. 'You're kneeling on my neck.'

'It's got her,' squeaked Will. 'In the front yard. A vampire's got Shelley and it's eating her blood.'

Corey closed his eyes. Maybe he was still asleep. Maybe if he tried really hard, he could have a dream about the ice-cream cake Mum and Dad got him last week for his tenth birthday. Maybe he could taste again those three delicious flavours in the shape of Stadium Australia.

'If you don't wake up,' said Will, 'I'll tell Mum how you stayed in bed and let a vampire get Shelley while she was supposed to be babysitting us.'

Corey groaned again.

He got up. He didn't have any choice. Will was dragging him by his bottom lip.

They stumbled to the window.

Will wrestled open the curtain. Corey helped him. Will pointed down into the front yard.

'See?'

Corey squinted. Mostly he could just see shadows. Then the moonlight went brighter and he saw Shelley leaning against the side of the carport.

Somebody was with her. Another teenager.

Corey shuddered. It was a fairly yukky sight.

Shelley had her arms wrapped around the teenager and the teenager's mouth was on her neck.

'I think it's Draclia,' whispered Will, his breath hot in Corey's ear.

Corey sighed.

'The word is Dracula,' he said. 'And that's not Dracula, that's Jarrod Bennet.'

Will didn't look convinced.

'Jarrod Bennet's in high school with Shelley,' said Corey. 'His younger sister Brianna goes to our school.'

Will thought about this.

'Does Brianna know her brother's a vampire who bites people on the neck?' asked Will.

Corey sat down wearily on his bed.

He tried to explain to Will that Shelley and Jarrod were just kissing. That because Shelley was very tall for her age, Jarrod couldn't reach her lips, not even on tiptoe, and he had to make do with her neck.

Will still didn't look convinced.

Corey realised it was all probably a bit technical for a five year old.

He decided to keep it simple.

'Jarrod is Shelley's boyfriend,' he explained.

'They've been going out for nearly a week.'

'Vampires just pretend to be your boyfriend,' said Will. 'I saw it on telly.'

Corey sighed again.

You couldn't really blame a little kid. Not in a world gone vampire mad. There had hardly been a day in Will's young life without a new vampire romance book being published or a vampire movie being released or a vampire TV series being launched or a vampire burger being advertised on the car radio.

Little kids noticed things like that.

Corey had done the same when he was small and the world had been dinosaur mad. For a few weeks when he was five, Corey had seriously suspected there were dinosaurs trapped in the ice under the frozen peas in Coles.

Corey made Will sit next to him on the bed.

'Vampires are just stories,' he said to Will.

His little brother shook his head.

'Vampires live among us,' muttered Will darkly. 'Shelley told me.'

Thanks Shelley, thought Corey. I hope I'm that thoughtful and considerate when I'm fifteen.

He looked at the clock.

Ten past ten. Mum and Dad probably wouldn't be back from book club till eleven.

Corey needed sleep now. Desperately. But he knew there was only one way he was going to get it.

'OK,' he said to Will. 'Come on. I'll prove to you that vampires are just stories.'

Shelley's room was full of vampires.

But, as Corey carefully pointed out to Will, none of them were real.

Shelley had about a hundred vampire love story books on her shelves. And DVDs and posters of hunky heart-throb teenage vampire guys and plastic models of them and a *Twilight* bedcover.

'See,' said Corey. 'Vampires are just pretend.'

'Mum's got heaps of gardening books,' said Will, 'and gardening's real.'

Corey took a deep breath.

'Look,' he said, 'even if there was such a thing as vampires, which there isn't, Shelley wouldn't go out with one. She can be a bit bossy at times, but she's not stupid.'

'She would so go out with one,' said Will. 'She told me. She likes vampire boyfriends. All her friends do.'

Corey stared at the *Twilight* bedcover.

It's all that movie's fault, he thought bitterly. I wish I had the phone numbers of the people who made that movie and all those books. I'd make them come round and stay up half the night arguing with Will, so I could get some sleep.

'Anyway,' said Will. 'Draclia makes you be his girl-friend. I saw it on a cartoon.'

Corey opened his mouth to remind Will that (a) information from cartoons isn't that reliable and (b) the word is Dracula.

Before he could, Shelley burst into the room.

'What are you doing in here?' she said, glaring at them.

'Um,' said Corey. 'We couldn't sleep.'

'Out,' said Shelley.

'We've come to save you,' said Will. 'From Draclia.'

Shelley rolled her eyes angrily and gave Corey a 'grow up' look. Which Corey felt was very unfair as he was grown up, almost. Will was the little kid with the dopey ideas.

'I was just trying to explain something to Will,' he said. 'He's got some dopey idea about Jarrod. Of course it's completely . . .'

Corey didn't finish. Shelley grabbed the front of his pyjama top and twisted it so tight he could hardly breathe, let alone finish sentences.

'Stay away from Jarrod,' hissed Shelley, eyes blazing. 'If you do anything to upset him, you're dead meat, both of you.'

Even though his brain was struggling for oxygen, and he was concerned about Will who looked close to tears, Corey was still able to work out almost instantly why Shelley was being so yukky.

It was her height.

Teenage boys didn't like teenage girls who were taller than them, not as girlfriends. Shelley had said that tearfully a million times.

But now, at last, she'd found one who didn't mind. So of course she didn't want him driven away by a loony five-year-old vampire hunter and a not very good babysitter brother.

Corey could understand that.

The thing he couldn't understand, now Shelley

had pulled him even closer and he could see her skin in more detail, was why she had blood smeared on her neck.

'Corey, wake up. Corey, wake up. Wake up, Corey.'

Corey woke up.

Will's face was touching his. It was sticky. Corey could smell milk and cornflakes and truck plastic.

'Draclia's in the kitchen,' whispered Will urgently.

Corey closed his eyes. The early morning sunlight was hurting his head. So was Will's voice. For a moment he wondered if Will was a vampire. A sleep vampire who took all your sleep.

'In our kitchen,' said Will, even more urgently.

'Go and keep him busy,' mumbled Corey. 'Show him your truck. Don't let him leave. And don't say anything about vampires. I'll be down soon.'

'OK,' said Will, and hurried off.

Corey was tempted to go back to sleep. But he didn't. He had to fix this once and for all. Put Will's mind at rest. For Will's sake and for Shelley's.

In the shower Corey made a list in his mind of all the things he knew about vampires.

1. They hate sunlight.

2. They hate having wooden stakes stuck in them.

3. They hate garlic.

4. Sometimes they can turn into bats.

Right, thought Corey as he went down to the kitchen. I must be able to use at least one of these to prove to Will that Jarrod Bennet is not a vampire.

Mum and Dad and Will were at the kitchen table.

Nobody else was.

'Where's Shelley?' asked Corey casually. 'And, um, Jarrod?'

'Don't know,' said Dad. 'They were here a moment ago, then they just sort of vanished.'

'Shelley wouldn't let me show Draclia my truck,' said Will bitterly.

Corey sighed. Will was glaring at the chair Jarrod must have been sitting in. Which was empty now except for a cricket bat.

A cricket bat?

Corey stared at the bat, mind racing.

Could vampires turn into that sort of bat?

He shook the thought away and told himself to stop being silly. This wasn't helping anyone.

'I think they've gone to the mall,' said Mum.

'I asked them if they wanted to watch me play in the over-forties cricket,' said Dad. 'But they weren't interested.'

'Yes they were, love,' said Mum. 'But Jarrod's got very sensitive skin. He doesn't like being in the sun.'

Corey told his imagination to calm down. You're ten years old, he told it. You know how the world works. You know that lots of people have sensitive skin. Some people even have such sensitive skin that too much kissing can make it leak.

'What are you planning to do today, Corey?' said Mum.

'Um,' said Corey. 'I'm going to Brianna Bennet's house to do a scientific experiment. I can take Will if you like. I think he'll be interested.'

'Yes,' shrieked Will. 'I love scientific speriments. I'm a vampire for scientific speriments.'

'The Bennets live next to the cemetery, right?' said Dad.

Corey nodded.

'Go the long way round the block,' said Mum. 'So you don't have to cross any roads.'

Corey nodded again.

He was only half listening.

Mostly he was wondering if Mum had any garlic.

'Why don't we just ring the bell?' said Will.

Corey dragged Will back down into the bushes in the Bennets' front yard.

'Because,' whispered Corey, 'we can't just stand at the front door and say hello Mrs Bennet, we've come to hide a lump of garlic in Jarrod's bed so that if he starts foaming at the mouth or writhing around on the floor or not being able to concentrate on his homework we'll know he's a vampire.'

'Why not?' said Will.

Corey took a deep breath.

He decided to keep it simple.

'Because,' he said, 'it's more fun to climb in through Jarrod's bedroom window.'

'Yes,' shrieked Will, muffled by the hand that Corey slapped over his mouth with the speed of a, well, vampire.

Luckily the Bennets' house was single storey, and Jarrod's room was easy to spot. Shelley had been telling everyone for days that Jarrod had black curtains.

What Shelley hadn't told anyone, Corey discovered, was that Jarrod also had a really sharp flyscreen that cut your finger when you took it off the window.

'Ow,' said Corey, sucking his finger.

'Don't let it bleed,' said Will. 'If Jarrod smells your blood he'll go into a frenzy and want to marry you.'

Corey didn't think there was a huge chance of that happening.

He concentrated on sliding Jarrod's window open as quietly as he could, then helping Will climb through. It took a while because Will had his school backpack on, which got wedged in the window.

Corey muttered some cross things very quietly and pushed as hard as he could. Suddenly Will and the backpack tumbled forward onto Jarrod's bed. Corey climbed through after him.

'Why did you bring your backpack?' he whispered, helping Will off the bed. 'You don't need your truck for vampire hunting.'

'It's not my truck,' said Will indignantly. 'It's a stake.'

Corey stared at him.

'A stake for vampire hunting,' said Will. 'If you jab

a stake into a vampire, they —'

'I know,' said Corey hurriedly.

He was shocked that Will even knew about this, let alone was planning to do it. And where had he got the stake anyway?

Corey slid the backpack off Will's back.

Best if I look after it, he thought. That's all we need now, a five year old running riot with a piece of sharp wood.

Corey froze.

Blood was dripping from the bottom of the backpack onto Jarrod's floor.

Corey stared, horrified.

Had the stake already been used?

Frantically he fumbled with the backpack zip, jerked it open and pulled out what was inside.

A torn plastic bag with raw meat in it.

'I told you,' said Will. 'It's a steak. I got it from the fridge at home. If you jab a steak into a vampire . . .'

'Not a steak,' said Corey weakly. 'A stake.'

'That's right,' said Will. 'A steak.'

'Jarrod, is that you?' called a grown-up voice outside the door.

Corey froze again. He gave Will a pleading look to make him stay still. He tried to stay completely still himself. Which wasn't easy because he had blood trickling along his arm.

The door opened.

Mrs Bennet put her head in and stared, surprised.

'Hello,' said Corey weakly.

Mrs Bennet stared at him some more.

'You're Shelley's brother, right?' she said.

'Yes,' said Will. He pointed to Corey. 'So's he.'

Mrs Bennet was looking at the dripping steak in Corey's hand.

Corey tried to work out how he was going to explain to Mrs Bennet (1) why he and Will were in her son's bedroom doing a vampire hunt, and (2) why they were doing it in such a stupid way.

'Oh, silly me,' said Mrs Bennet, suddenly smiling. 'Of course. Jarrod must have invited you to lunch.'

Will gave a terrified squeak.

Corey wasn't sure what to say.

'Your mum needn't have bothered with this,' said Mrs Bennet warmly, taking the meat from Corey. 'My husband always gets too much steak for our barbecues.

Come on through. Brianna and the others will be pleased to see you.'

Corey grabbed Will's hand and they followed Mrs Bennet out to the back patio.

'Look who's here,' said Mrs Bennet to the people sitting around the table.

Everyone turned and stared at Corey and Will.

Mr Bennet and Brianna looked pleased.

Jarrod looked confused.

Shelley looked cross.

'They even brought their own meat,' said Mrs Bennet.

Nobody else said anything. Everyone just kept on smiling, or frowning, or scowling at Corey and Will.

Corey decided he should say something.

'And our own garlic,' he said.

At first it was quite a tense barbecue.

Particularly for Will and Shelley. Corey could see they were extremely tense. Will kept glancing nervously at Jarrod, and Shelley kept glancing nervously at Corey and Will.

Corey decided to help everyone relax.

'Vampires,' he said. 'You can't get away from them these days, can you?'

Everyone looked at bit startled at first.

Corey had to hold Will's hand tight under the table to keep him there.

But soon everyone was talking about their favourite vampire movies and TV shows and books. Even Shelley started to relax.

Corey chose his moment.

'Sorry we went into your room,' he said to Jarrod.

'My room?' said Jarrod, looking confused again.

'I did it for Will,' said Corey. 'To show him that real life is different to the movies. Lucky your bed was there to break our fall. And lucky it's a strong bed. With strong bedsprings. In your bed.'

He hoped he'd said it enough for Will to get the message.

'That bed needs to be strong,' said Mrs Bennet. 'The number of hours Jarrod sleeps.'

Thank you, said Corey silently.

'Twelve hours a night, if they let him,' said Brianna.

Thank you too, said Corey silently again.

'Easy to see Jarrod's not a vampire,' he said, out loud.

Everyone looked at Corey.

Corey realised he hadn't explained enough.

''Cause vampires don't sleep,' he said. 'Not ever. Not at all. Not even when their eyes are closed.'

Everyone laughed. Including Shelley. And when Corey glanced across at Will, he was grinning too.

Corey felt weak with relief.

Problem solved, except for one little thing.

Corey had barely thought of it, when it got solved as well.

'OK, time to eat,' said Mrs Bennet. 'Jarrod, get rid of that revolting gum, please.'

Jarrod stuck something on the edge of his plate.

Red bubblegum.

Of course, thought Corey. The red smears on Shelley's neck. They weren't blood, they were bubble-gum juice.

He felt happier than he had for ages. Happy that Shelley had managed to find a boyfriend at last. Happy that Jarrod's family were so nice and friendly and mortal. Happy that with a bit of luck Will would stop carrying on like an insomniac Transylvanian innkeeper and let him get some sleep.

Then Mr Bennet brought the steaks over from the barbecue.

Corey stared.

They were barely cooked. The outsides were sort of scorched, but the insides were still red.

'We aways have our steak rare,' said Mr Bennet. 'Hope you like it that way.'

Mrs Bennet plonked a steak on Corey's plate.

'There you go,' she said. 'Folk who climb in through windows have to keep their strength up.'

Corey felt faint.

He hadn't even cut his steak yet, and a puddle of blood was trickling out of it. What could he do? Everyone thought he and Will had come to lunch. You couldn't come to lunch and not eat the lunch.

Corey cut off a small piece of steak. He tried not to look at the blood. He put the piece of steak into his mouth and hoped he wouldn't throw up.

He didn't.

The steak was delicious.

He had another piece.

This was incredible. It looked revolting but tasted fantastic. The mixture of crisp burnt outside and tender juicy inside was the best thing he'd ever tasted that wasn't in the shape of Stadium Australia.

Corey had more.

Then he remembered Will. He turned to his brother.

Will was eating even faster than Corey. His eyes were shining as he chewed. He grinned at Corey, lips red and gleaming.

Corey grinned back.

He looked around the table. Everyone was doing the same as Will.

'Good, eh?' said Mr Bennet.

Everyone nodded, mouths full.

Corey put another big, tender, dripping chunk of meat into his mouth and chewed happily.

Then he had a little nagging thought and stopped.

Was this how it started? he wondered.

He reached over to the dish of fried garlic and scooped up a spoonful and sprinkled it over the rest of his steak before he put the next big chunk into his mouth.

Just in case.

Tickled Onions

I hate doing this, but every morning I have to.

The other kids call it Clyde Craddock's mental moment.

As soon as I arrive at school, I hurry over to the garbage skip behind the canteen. First I check in the skip for leftover bread from yesterday, because by 8.45 in the morning I'm always starving.

Then I pull the plastic bag out of my pocket, careful not to spill what's inside it.

Soggy muesli with sun-dried tomatoes. Or maybe a sour plum and choko yoghurt pancake. Or seafood sausages with pig liver marmalade. Or whatever else we had for breakfast at our place.

I always feel guilty as I dump my breakfast in the skip, because I know it was cooked with love. Mum and Dad are the most loving parents in the world. They're just not that good at listening.

After I've dumped my breakfast, I reach into my school bag, take out my lunch box, open the lid carefully, try not to breathe in the revolting smell, and dump my lunch too.

Today's smell is even worse than usual.

It's partly the salami mousse sandwich, which is one of Mum's favourites.

But mostly it's the tickled onions.

That's what Dad calls them, and I suppose he's allowed to because he invented them. They're like regular pickled onions except for the rose petals and chilli powder and fermented fish paste.

Into the garbage they go.

Some of the kids from my class are watching me and giggling.

'Mental,' I hear a couple of them whisper as usual.

I sigh as usual.

I don't really mind. Not that much. I'm used to it. And you'd think the other kids would be as well.

I've been doing this since year one and we're in year six now.

I live in hope that one day I'll hear them whisper something else. Something like, 'Poor Clyde, it must be really hard for him, having parents whose hobby is amateur cooking.'

That would be amazing.

I'd really like that.

Oh well, at least my morning routine isn't as bad as Hamish Hodge's. At least I don't have to actually eat this muck.

Not like poor Hamish.

Here he comes now, with Rick, Jock, Mick, Jack and Vic.

Oh no, they're twisting Hamish's arms even further up his back than they usually do.

I wish they'd grow up. Most of us year sixes are in the footy club or the movie club or the phone club. But Rick, Jock, Mick, Jack and Vic had to be different. They had to start a club called Overweight Watchers. A whole club just to make fun of overweight people. And the only overweight person in year six is Hamish Hodge.

'Hodge Podge delivery,' the club members are crowing like they do every morning. 'Starving fat boy coming through. Hasn't eaten for ten minutes. Needs to see what's on the breakfast menu.'

This is usually when I turn away.

It's not just the horrible sight of Hamish having his head forced into the skip. It's the look he usually gives me before it happens. A look that says, 'If only you'd eat your breakfast, I wouldn't have to.'

But today I'm not turning away. I'm stepping closer to Rick, Jock, Mick, Jack and Vic.

'Hey,' I say. 'Lay off him.'

What's going on? Hunger must be scrambling my brain.

Rick, Jock, Mick, Jack and Vic turn to me. They don't look pleased. They're all big, specially Vic who does weight-lifting as part of her netball training.

I'm quite tall, but I don't have much meat on my bones. It's not surprising, seeing as I live on one meal a day, which is whatever sandwiches I can get from kids in return for doing their homework.

'Oh yeah, Creepy Craddock?' says Jock, glaring at me. 'Hodge Podge a friend of yours, is he?'

Hamish Hodge is looking at me as well, eyes wide. He's got two different expressions on his plump face at once. Hope that I'll save him and worry that I'll make things worse.

I've started this now, so I have to finish it. Dad says it's important to finish what you start, though he's usually talking about food.

'Yeah,' I say. 'Me and Hamish are good friends. I'm going to his place for tea tonight.'

Rick, Jock, Mick, Jack and Vic look surprised.

So does Hamish.

Then all the others smirk.

'I'd like to see that,' says Vic. 'A loony who chucks his food in the bin having tea with a fatso who can't stop eating.'

They all have a big laugh.

Until Jock stops and gets serious.

'And why exactly should we lay off Hodge Podge?' he says, sticking his face close to mine. 'Is it because you're gunna make us?'

The smell of bacon on Jock's breath is making me feel faint with hunger. But I manage to remember what I need to say.

I look Jock right in the eyes.

'PD project,' I say.

Jock frowns. Rick, Mick, Jack and Vic glance at each other. Slowly they realise what I mean.

Ms Dunphy has just set a really difficult Personal Development project. It's on Empathy. Four hundred words on Other People's Feelings, by next Tuesday.

Rick, Jock, Mick, Jack and Vic need help.

'If we let the fat boy go,' says Jock, 'we're not giving you sandwiches as well.'

'Done,' I say.

The Overweight Watchers club members look at each other, nod, scowl at me, scowl at Hamish, and wander away.

Hamish is panting with relief.

'Thanks,' he says. 'I thought I was going to have to eat those stinky horrible onions again.'

He remembers where the onions come from.

'Sorry,' he says. 'I didn't mean to insult your parents.'

'That's OK,' I say. 'You can make it up to me with a delicious meal tonight.'

Hamish stares at me, alarmed.

'Were you serious about coming to tea?' he says.

'Of course,' I say. 'I don't joke about food. Food is the most important thing in my life. I haven't had a decent meal since I was four.'

While we walk to his place after school, Hamish tells me a bit about himself. We've never really had a chance to talk much. He's only been at the school eight months and he's spent a lot of that time with his head in the skip.

'I wasn't always porky,' he says. 'I used to be almost as skinny as you.'

'What happened?' I say.

I heard somewhere that thyroid glands, whatever they are, can make people fat. Probaby depends how they're cooked.

'My mum died,' says Hamish.

I give him a sympathetic look. It's moments like this you realise food isn't the most important thing.

Not quite.

'My dad's in charge of meals now,' says Hamish gloomily. 'He likes huge meals. Every day.'

This sounds promising.

'What's for tea tonight?' I say.

'Dunno,' says Hamish. 'Could be anything.'

I smile.

It could be anything, but I'm pretty confident it won't be seafood sausages with pig liver marmalade.

Hamish's house is nice. Bit like ours, but tidier.

As we come in, a man's voice calls out.

'Nearly finished, Hamie. Get yourself a snack.'

We go into the kitchen. Hamish explains that his dad is a freelance journalist who works at home. I nod, but I'm not fully paying attention. I've just noticed something that's making me feel nervous.

There's no food in the kitchen.

In our kitchen there are jars and packets stacked everywhere, and stuff hanging up all over the place. Chillies and herbs and bits of dried goat. It's all yuk, but there's heaps of it.

Here, nothing.

Hamish opens the fridge and takes out a bottle of water.

I peek in while the door's open. I see a few bits of fruit, half a packet of cheese and a jar of ointment.

Where are the huge meals?

'Hi there, Hamie,' says Hamish's dad behind us. 'Who's this?'

Hamish's dad is exactly the same shape as Hamish. Not blubbery or anything, but happily plump. I'd like to be that shape.

Hamish introduces me.

'Clyde's my best friend at school,' he says.

I try to look as though I am. Which isn't hard because I don't think Hamish has got any other friends.

'Can Clyde eat with us tonight?' Hamish says to his dad.

Mr Hodge looks me up and down.

'Looks like he needs to,' he chuckles. 'We're going to a steakhouse. That OK with you, Clyde?'

I nod so hard I get giddy.

'Right-oh then,' says Mr Hodge. 'Let's give your folks a call.'

I can't believe it.

This steakhouse menu is amazing.

Most of the steaks are half a kilo at least. And this place obviously hasn't even heard of pig liver marmalade.

The ony thing I'm a bit worried about is the prices. I don't want to send Mr Hodge broke.

Mr Hodge looks up from his menu.

'OK, boys,' he says. 'What are you having? Anything you like.'

I glance uncertainly across the table at Hamish.

'It's OK,' says Hamish quietly. 'The magazine's paying.'

I'm not sure what he means.

'My dad does restaurant reviews,' explains Hamish. 'Two a week for a magazine, plus five for their website.'

'Seven restaurants a week,' says Mr Hodge. He grins. 'Lucky we get seven dinnertimes a week, eh?'

'Yeah,' says Hamish miserably. 'Very lucky.'

'I'm doing a book, too,' says Mr Hodge. '*One Thousand And One Restaurants You Must Visit Before You Diet.*'

Hamish rolls his eyes.

'Only joking,' says Mr Hodge. 'Now, what do you like the look of?'

'Um,' I say, trying not to speak too fast, 'can I have the eight hundred and fifty gram Ridiculously Rotund Rump, please?'

'You sure can,' says Mr Hodge. 'I'm having the

Ludicrously Large Lamb Fillet, so Hamie, would you mind having the Colossal Kilo T-Bone so you can tell me what it's like?'

Hamish nods unhappily.

His dad is studying the menu again and doesn't notice.

'Right,' says Mr Hodge. 'We need to have a starter each, two if you can manage it. And lots of side serves. Fries, onion rings, wedges, nachos. OK?'

Hamish doesn't say anything, so I answer for us both.

'OK,' I say, grinning.

'Thanks for last night,' says Hamish the next morning.

I look up from the skip, where I'm dumping a bag of particularly revolting scrambled eggs. The smell of the sardines and vinegar in the eggs is making my eyes water, so I can't see if Hamish is being sarcastic.

My eyes clear and I see he isn't.

I also see that Rick, Jock, Mick, Jack and Vic aren't with him. I'm glad about that.

'Thank you,' I say to Hamish. 'It was the best meal of my life.'

'Dunno how you did it,' says Hamish, 'eating all

the side serves and three desserts and half my T-bone as well as your steak, but thanks.'

'My pleasure,' I say, tossing a dried goat and curdled whey sourdough sandwich into the skip.

A shadow falls over us.

Five shadows, actually.

Before Rick, Jock, Mick, Jack and Vic can get started, I reach into my bag and pull out a sheet of paper.

'I've done you some project notes,' I say. 'Just some basic stuff about other people's feelings, what they are, how they work, how to spot them, stuff like that.'

Jock snatches the sheet of paper. Rick, Mick, Jack and Vic huddle around him and squint at it.

'I'll do some more tomorrow,' I say.

The weight-mocking club glare at me and leave.

Hamish is looking at me. I can see there's something he wants to say. I assume it's 'thank you', but it turns out to be something slightly different.

'Clyde,' he says. 'Do you want to have tea with us again tonight?'

'Good word, "yummy",' says Mr Hodge, opening his notebook on the restaurant table and jotting my word down. 'I don't use that word enough. What about the roast chicken? How would you describe that?'

I use a different word because I figure that's what a journalist would want.

'Delish,' I say.

'Good,' says Mr Hodge, writing again. 'What about you, Hamie?'

'I didn't have any chicken, Dad,' says Hamish.

'No problem,' says Mr Hodge. 'The lamb chops?'

'I didn't have any of those either,' says Hamish.

'Simple and scrumptious,' I say.

I describe the fish as 'no nonsense', the veggies as 'superbly recognisable' and the apple tart as 'not mucked around with'.

'Good on you, Clyde,' says Mr Hodge. 'You're the perfect professional dining companion. And well done, Hamie, for making such a spot-on best friend.'

'You're welcome,' says Hamish quietly.

Mr Hodge looks at me.

'If I have a word with your folks,' he says, 'would you like to eat with us every night?'

I hesitate for a moment. Only because I'm a bit worried about our dog Garnish. Usually I take him for a walk each evening so I can slip him my dinner. He's missed out for the last two nights. All he's had is the regular dog food Mum gives him. But now that I think about it, he's probably better off. Look how much happier Hamish is now that he's eating less.

I glance at Hamish. He seems pretty pleased his dad's made the offer.

'Thank you,' I say to Mr Hodge. 'I'd like that heaps.'

'Right-oh,' says Mr Hodge. 'I'll call your folks later. Now I need to check out the washroom. A restaurant reviewer's work is never done.'

After his dad has gone, Hamish's face falls.

He gives a big sigh.

'Don't worry,' I say. 'I don't have to eat with you every night. Not every single night. Not if you don't want me to.'

I already have a plan. If I bring a couple of my plastic bags with me when I do eat with Hamish and his dad, I can stock up for the nights I don't.

'It's not that,' says Hamish. 'I really like having you around. And I'm very grateful for how much of my food you eat. I've lost two kilos in the last two days.'

I'm puzzled. Hamish looks like he's about to cry.

'I just hate having a dad who's a restaurant reviewer,' says Hamish. 'I just wish me and Dad could have a normal meal at home each night.'

I stare at Hamish. I can't believe what I'm hearing. Hamish is like a lottery winner who wishes he hadn't bought the ticket.

'We've been doing this so long,' says Hamish, 'I think Dad's forgotten what a normal meal at home is.'

Hamish hesitates. He has that look he gets when there's something he wants to ask but he's not sure how. Even before he spits it out, I guess what it is.

Oh no.

'Clyde,' says Hamish, 'could you invite us to your place for tea one night? So my dad can see how normal people do it? So when I ask him to give up his job he'll understand?'

I open my mouth to tell Hamish what a really bad idea that is. How only an idiot would ask a dad to give up the best job in the world. And how tea at my place is about as far from normal as you can get without going into outer space and eating whatever grows there.

But I don't say it.

Maybe it's Hamish's miserable face, or maybe it's

Ms Dunphy's class project, but suddenly I'm putting myself in Hamish's shoes.

No mum.

Body shape a whole club has been formed to mock.

Only one friend in the whole world.

And even though the chicken and fish and lamb in my tummy have turned themselves into an anxiety burger, I invite Hamish and his dad to tea at our place.

'Come in,' says Mum with a big smile a couple of nights later. 'You must be Hamish.'

I introduce Hamish and Mr Hodge to Mum and Dad and Garnish.

We all go into the lounge.

'Peanut?' says Dad, once we're all sitting down.

My tummy goes tense. But it's OK, Mum and Dad are sticking to what they promised. No home-roasted peanuts with curried prawn paste and fermented kelp. Just normal ones with salt out of a supermarket packet.

I can see Mr Hodge thinks they're a bit boring.

Hamish loves them. Well, loves it, because he's only having one.

'Chip?' says Dad.

I go tense again, but it's still OK. They're normal chips out of a crinkly packet, normal flavour, not even a hint of intestine.

It's amazing. I gave up trying to make Mum and Dad listen to me years ago. But yesterday, when I explained to them why tonight had to be normal, they actually heard me. I don't know how I did it. Maybe when we're trying to help a friend who really needs us, we get more determined.

I'll have to suggest that to Ms Dunphy as a subject for a project.

Anyway, Mum and Dad are doing really well.

We're having a nice normal evening.

So far.

'Let's eat,' says Mum.

OK, that's not so normal. I don't think hostesses normally herd guests over to the dinner table four minutes after they arrive. I think Mum must be feeling a bit stressed by the effort of serving a normal meal.

We go into the kitchen.

Our dining table has been in the kitchen for years. Mum and Dad like to have it close to the stove because a lot of what they cook congeals very quickly.

I glance anxiously around the kitchen. Everything's been packed away in cupboards, or under our beds. Except for the dried goat strips, which are hanging in my wardrobe.

'Hope you like roast lamb, Charles,' says Mum to Mr Hodge.

'I do, thanks,' he says.

I think he's starting to relax. He's not quite as enthusiastic as when he's reading a restaurant menu, but he looks pretty happy.

Hamish is glowing with happiness.

Mum takes dinner out of the oven. It's exactly what she said. Normal roast lamb. No stuffing, no crust, no bone marrow sauce with pickled fungus.

Dad carves.

Mum puts the veggies on the table. Roast potatoes. Peas. Carrots.

I have a moment of anxiety about the gravy. But it's OK. It's out of a packet.

'Mmmm,' says Mr Hodge. 'That looks amazing.'

I grin at Hamish. He grins back.

We're both about to have the best meal of our lives.

Then I notice that the thing Mr Hodge is staring

at, the thing he just said was amazing, isn't the lamb. Or the veggies.

He's looking up at the shelf over the fridge. At the one thing, I now see, that me and Mum and Dad forgot to pack away.

A jar of tickled onions.

'What unusual onions,' says Mr Hodge.

I'm not surprised he says that. You don't often see onions that have turned purple.

Mr Hodge gets up and goes over to the shelf.

'May I?' he says.

Mum and Dad don't say anything. I haven't got a clue what their thoughts are right now or their feelings, and I've done a project on the subject.

Mr Hodge lifts the jar down, unscrews the lid, takes out a tickled onion, and puts it into his mouth.

Hamish is looking worried.

I'm feeling the same. I try to tell myself that one unusual food item doesn't stop a meal from being normal.

'Incredible,' says Mr Hodge when he's finished crunching the tickled onion. 'Fermented fish paste, right? And chilli. And rose petals. Where did you get these delicious onions?'

Mum and Dad look at each other.

I can see exactly what they're feeling now. Even Rick, Jock, Mick, Jack and Vic could spot this much pride.

'We made them,' said Mum.

'Amazing,' says Mr Hodge.

'We're quite keen amateur cooks,' says Dad.

Before I can stop anyone, Dad opens the fridge and Mr Hodge is tasting pig liver marmalade and jellied goat curd tarts and a whole lot of other stuff, with Garnish panting hopefully at his feet.

Mr Hodge looks like he's having the best night of his life.

'What is this incredibly delicious thing I'm eating now?' he says.

'Salami mousse,' says Mum.

Mr Hodge sits back down at the table, deep in thought. He thinks for quite a while. I wonder if he's thinking about why on earth anyone would make mousse out of salami. Probably not.

Then he speaks, gazing at Mum and Dad, his eyes shining.

'Stephanie,' he says. 'Neil. Have you ever thought of opening a restaurant?'

There's a stunned silence.

Except for the soft sound of Hamish sobbing.

'Come on boys, your tucker's on the table.'

Me and Hamish don't need to be told twice. We dump our ping-pong bats and dash to the dinner table.

Yum. Veggie soup.

Mrs Walsh makes the best veggie soup in the world. Her secret is she puts bits of grilled steak in it.

Hamish tucks in. Since Mum and Dad and Mr Hodge opened their restaurant, and hired the best housekeeper in the world to look after me and Hamish, he looks forward to tea at home every night.

So do I.

'Dad's here,' says Hamish happily as a car door slams.

Mr Hodge comes home from the restaurant for an hour each evening to have tea with us.

That's only fair, because Mum and Dad have breakfast with us each morning. They don't have to be at Tickled Onions, which is what their restaurant is called, until the first deliveries arrive at ten. Though sometimes the pig livers are delivered earlier.

'Is that veggie soup?' says Mr Hodge, joining us at the table. 'Delish. I'll have a large serve, thanks Mrs Walsh. It's soup, so it's not fattening.'

We all grin.

Mr Hodge has trimmed down a bit since he became a waiter. He reckons he walks twenty kilometres a night in the restaurant. Twenty-five if lots of customers ask for extra pig liver marmalade.

Hamish reckons he and his dad and me will all be the same shape soon.

It's possible, though modern science reckons body shape is partly genetic and metabolic, as I explained to Rick, Jock, Mick, Jack and Vic in the project notes I gave them this morning.

At first they didn't want the notes.

They were more interested in having what was in my lunch box. I think they could smell Mrs Walsh's pickled onions. But I was hanging on to those.

Mrs Walsh makes them the normal way, and they're delicious.

Secret Diary of a Dad

Sunday, 3 January

Not a good day.

'Dad,' said the kids this morning, 'why are you kneeling on the floor with your head in the fridge? Have you got a headache?'

I explained I hadn't, I was just telling the tops of the plastic salad containers about my school days.

Maddy and Dylan stared at me.

Nine year olds and seven year olds can be a bit slow sometimes.

'It's one of my New Year resolutions,' I explained, showing them the list I'd made. 'See? Number four.'

'*Spend more time talking to the kids*,' read Maddy.

I took the list back.

'Does it say kids?' I said, peering at it. 'I could have sworn it said lids.'

The kids sighed. So did the lids.

'Pity you haven't kept the first New Year resolution on your list,' said Dylan.

'I have,' I said, squeaking to my feet and showing them my bright-yellow rubber footwear. 'See? *Get new galoshes.*'

The kids sighed again. 'Dad,' they groaned, pointing to the list, 'it says *get new glasses.*'

'Oh dear,' I said, squinting at the blurry writing. A chill crept up my spine and not just because I'd left the fridge door open. 'Um,' I said, 'I'm feeling a bit worried now about New Year resolutions two and three.'

The kids studied the list. 'Two,' they read, '*polish the car.* What's wrong with that?'

I took them outside and pointed up to the roof of the house.

'There's no car up there,' said the kids.

Then they saw the shiny cat.

The cat slid off the roof, leaving a trail of Supa-Shine

wax on the tiles. The kids caught it, glared at me and we went inside.

'Number three can't be worse than that,' said Maddy.

I could feel a headache coming on, so I put my head in the fridge. The kids read out number three.

'*Get more sleep.* What's so bad about that?'

I closed my eyes, laid my head down next to the lettuce and waited for them to hear the baaing coming from the living room.

Wednesday, 6 January

I'm feeling very proud today.

Actually, the feeling started a couple of days ago, when I finally found my glasses and built my first ever piece of furniture. OK, it wasn't perfect, but I did it without help and I was proud of myself. I could feel my chest swelling almost as much as the finger I'd hit with the hammer.

'Well?' I said to the kids when they came to look. 'What do you think?'

I held my breath as they ran their hands over the four sturdy legs, the finely stitched upholstery and the skilfully hung mirrored door.

'Funny-looking bookshelves, Dad,' they said.

My chest deflated. They were right. Who was I kidding? I've always been a hopeless handyman.

'Do-it-yourself furniture,' I said bitterly. 'If there's anyone who can actually build this stuff I'd like to know their secret.'

The kids looked at the empty boxes strewn around the room.

'Perhaps,' said Maddy gently, 'it involves assembling the bookcase, the settee, the coffee table and the bathroom cabinet as four separate items.'

Kids can be know-it-alls sometimes, specially when they're right.

'It was the stupid instructions,' I said. 'They were impossible to understand. Look at that diagram. I broke a screwdriver trying to follow that.'

The kids sighed.

'That's the furniture shop logo,' said Dylan.

I realised my problem was that I didn't speak the language of do-it-yourself. So I went to my local language school and enrolled.

'Which language would you like to learn?' said the receptionist. 'French? Spanish? Japanese?'

'Furniture Assembly,' I said.

The language instructor tried hard, but by the end of the day I still couldn't translate, 'Slot base support bracket A into side panel rib B.' I couldn't even say it.

'I'm sorry,' said the instructor. 'I can't do any more for you.'

I looked at him pleadingly. 'Not even put my bookshelves together?'

He shook his head.

At home, I stared gloomily at the impossible bookshelf assembly instructions. Why could I make other complicated things like sandwiches and hot chocolate with marshmallows, but not a piece of furniture?

Well, no point brooding.

I slid the instruction booklet into the row of books on the bookshelf and turned away sadly.

Hang on.

I turned back.

The bookshelves were built. With base support brackets slotted into side support ribs and everything.

'We did it while you were at the language school,' said Maddy.

'It was actually quite easy,' said Dylan.

I stared at them, amazed. I gave them both a big hug. Incredible. My own kids can build furniture.

I am so proud.

Tuesday, 12 January

Today I finally got a chance to take the kids somewhere I've wanted to take them for a long time.

'If you think the green mould down the back of the fridge is amazing,' I said to them, 'wait till you see a rainforest.'

'Are you sure you don't want to come with us, Mum?' said Maddy as we set off.

'No thanks, my loves,' said Dawn, settling down on the motel verandah with a book. 'Have a good time.'

In the car I could see the kids were puzzled how anyone could prefer reading a first-aid book to visiting nature. I didn't blame them. They're only seven and nine. I'm their dad and I didn't get it either.

Or at least I didn't then.

I parked the car in the rainforest carpark.

'OK,' I whispered to the kids as we crept into the awesome green cathedral of trees and ferns. 'I want you to remember this is a very fragile place. Be gentle and respectful and don't touch anything. Let's just stand absolutely still for a moment and listen to the sound of nature in harmony, the delicate balance of a beautiful forest unspoiled by the destructive ways of man.'

'I wouldn't stand absolutely still if I was you,' said Maddy. 'A millipede the size of a comb has just run up your leg.'

I took her advice. I didn't stand still. I ran around in circles beating at my trousers with bracken and rubbing my bottom against several species of tree fern.

'You said we weren't allowed to touch anything,' said Dylan. 'You told us the rainforest is a fragile and delicate ecosystem and touching one leaf could muck it all up.'

'It is,' I said as I whacked at my upper thighs with a cedar log, 'and it could. Which is why I'm trying very hard not to touch any leaves.'

It wasn't easy.

I rolled around on the ground for a while, then reached inside my shirt, rummaged a bit, and pulled out a stag beetle the size of a telephone.

'Don't hurt it,' said the kids. 'And don't wave it around your head like that, you'll give it an upset tummy.'

The beetle finally released my arm from between its mandibles and scuttled away. Weak with relief, I tried to stand up. Something gave way underneath me.

'Dad,' said Dylan, 'do you think you should be sitting in that scorpions' nest?'

I didn't answer. I didn't want to disturb the big scorpion on my tongue.

'Also, Dad,' said Maddy, 'that's a rare stinkhorn fungus you're squashing. That foul-smelling slime is meant to be for the insects, not you.'

I spat the scorpion out and staggered to my feet.

'OK,' I said. 'Let's all calm down. Let's remember we're guests here in this idyllic paradise.'

I reached down to pick up my camera. It wasn't there. A large spider had just eaten it. The spider took a step towards me. It wanted my binoculars.

'Run,' I yelled to the kids.

We ran, crashing through the lush undergrowth. Leeches the size of drinking straws leapt up at us. Fruit-sucking moths the size of fruit swooped down on us.

Green pythons the size of green pythons (the big ones) stuck their tongues out at us.

'Wow,' said the kids. 'You didn't tell us rainforests were this exciting.'

Exhausted, dripping with sweat and that rather unpleasant substance double-eyed fig parrots exude from their bottoms, I collapsed onto a large moss-covered rock.

The rock moved. It was a giant tree frog looking for a tree that could support its weight.

'Arghhh,' I yelled. 'Please, don't hurt us, we're a protected species.'

We ran again. I led the way, sinking into swamps, struggling with giant ferns, wrestling my way past orchids that kept giving me karate kicks.

The kids stayed on the walking track. Finally we reached the carpark.

I hugged the car with relief for a while, then took a deep breath and turned to the kids.

'Well,' I said, 'there you have it. The tropical rainforest, nature's most precious gift to the planet.'

'And,' said Maddy, 'her most seriously threatened one.'

Dylan nodded in agreement.

'You're right,' I said. 'Even as we stand here, watching my ankles being nibbled by Herbert River ringtail possums, rainforests all over the world are being burned, chopped, mulched and bulldozed.'

The kids looked at me.

'Those things are awful, Dad,' they said, 'but they're not the biggest threat.'

I didn't understand what they meant.

They opened the car and made me sit inside it with a book. Then they went back into the rainforest without me.

Saturday, 16 January

Normally we all feel a bit down in the dumps at the end of a holiday, but not today. We're all very excited.

We've just got our first dog.

She arrived this morning. I think I was even more excited than the kids. The confusion. The noise. The joyful howls (the dog). The puddles on the carpet (me).

I've read all the dog care manuals, so I knew exactly what to do first.

Give her a feed.

'Better let us do that, Dad,' said the kids, taking the bowl. 'Better safe than sorry.'

I was indignant. The dog was indignant.

'Why?' I demanded.

'Because,' whispered Maddy so the dog wouldn't hear, 'you're hopeless with pets.'

I was deeply hurt.

'That goldfish,' I retorted, 'died of a bad cold.'

The kids looked at me sternly.

'It died,' said Dylan, 'because of what you fed it.'

I was even more indignant.

'The box had pictures of fish on it,' I said. 'How was I to know it was cat food?'

The kids looked sad. The dog looked nervous.

I took her for a walk round the block.

'We'll do that,' called the kids, running to catch up. 'Better safe than sorry.'

I boiled with indignation. The dog tried to hand them the lead.

'You're not being fair,' I said. 'I've never had a single accident taking a dog for a walk round the block. Or a fruit bat. Or a blue-tongue lizard.'

'That's right,' said Dylan sadly. 'Just a mouse. What

on earth possessed you to throw that stick and tell our mouse to fetch it?'

'With a hungry cat on the loose,' said Maddy. 'Whose dinner you'd just fed to the goldfish.'

Before I could answer, I realised I was holding an empty lead.

The dog had disappeared.

We found her halfway up a lamppost, trembling with fear.

The kids managed to coax her down, but only after I'd made a promise. That when I enrol the dog in training and obedience classes, I'll enrol as well. Ten weeks for the dog, twelve for me.

Sunday, 17 January

I try to be a good dad, but there are some skills I just don't have. Like watching TV while I'm being stared at. Specially by a dog with a lead in her mouth and two kids with cricket bats in theirs.

'Dad,' said the kids, 'you promised you'd take us to the park.'

'Wmpf,' agreed the dog.

'Don't talk with your mouths full,' I said, but they

were right, I had promised. 'We agreed we'd go after I've finished watching *The Bill*,' I reminded them.

'But Dad,' they wailed, 'we thought you meant one episode on telly, not two hundred and eighty-seven episodes on DVD.'

I sighed.

'Please,' I said. 'I'm trying to concentrate.'

I turned back to episode fifteen. Or was it sixteen? This was criminal.

'We'll go after I've finished watching *The Bill*,' I said firmly, 'and nothing you can say will make me change my mind.'

'Suit yourself,' said the kids. 'But if you don't get any exercise, you'll die.'

It was pouring with rain in the park, but I didn't care because I took a brilliant diving catch.

'Howzat!' I yelled triumphantly through the mud.

The umpire shook her head.

'Wmpf,' she said, licking her bottom.

On the way home I decided there must be a way to combine telly and exercise and mud-free nostrils.

That night I experimented.

'Who wants a lolly?' I asked, tossing one up and swinging my table-tennis bat.

It was a big success with the kids. They're such quick learners. When I told them they could have dinner in front of the TV, they just sat there with their mouths open so I could lob the rissoles in with a squash racket and whack the peas in with a golf club.

'Let him, Mum,' they squealed happily. 'It's exercise.'

My dear wife could see it was a good idea. She rolled her eyes in that loving way of hers. And later in the evening, when I sliced my shot with the pool cue and put a can of dog food through the TV screen in the middle of episode nineteen of *The Bill*, she smiled approvingly.

Thursday, 21 January

Our new goldfish arrived yesterday. And our new telly.

We all sat down and watched the news. There was a bit about how most men let their wives buy their clothes because they have no idea about fashion.

The family were looking at me and nodding. Which was unfair.

'I spilt sauce on my shirt at dinner,' I said. 'That's the only reason I'm wearing this green garbage bag.'

Today I decided to show them I do know about fashion. So I went shopping and bought myself a shirt. A very fashionable colourful bright one.

'Absolutely you, sir,' said the menswear assistant, putting on a second pair of sunglasses.

I squinted at my reflection. I looked like I'd just staggered out of an explosion in a paint factory.

'Are you sure?' I said.

'Computer screens have got millions of colours, right?' said the assistant. 'Well, this shirt's got even more millions. Definitely suits you, sir. The greens match your complexion.'

I wore it home. Cars swerved, buses ran into each other, and a light plane made a forced landing dragged down by the temporarily blinded birds clinging to its wings.

Not really. As if one shirt could cause a reaction like that.

Except at our place.

When I walked in, the whole family dived for cover, including the dog.

'Dad,' winced the kids, shielding their eyes with thick metal baking trays. 'Take it off. All the neighbours are closing their curtains.'

Patiently I explained that I was going to their school tonight for a parent–teacher meeting at the start of the new school year, and I was worried the teachers would lose interest and start chatting among themselves.

'Bright colours grab people's attention,' I said. 'Look at fire engines, and The Wiggles.'

'Dad,' sighed the kids, shielding the goldfish's eyes with lolly wrappers. 'When our teachers cop an eyeful of that shirt, they'll never be able to read another assignment.'

'Rubbish,' I said. 'Teachers are tough, specially round the eyeballs.'

I was right. At school tonight I had the teachers' attention from the moment I walked in.

Even before I said anything, every pair of eyes in the room was on me. Well, more on my shirt.

'So,' I said to the teachers. 'How's Dylan going with maths?'

They all just kept staring at the shirt. Their lips were

moving, but I don't think they were answering my question.

'Two million six hundred and forty-two thousand nine hundred and twenty-seven,' they were murmuring. 'Two million six hundred and forty-two thousand nine hundred and twenty-eight . . .'

Saturday, 23 January

The judge looked at me sternly. 'You have been charged,' he said, 'with one of the most serious crimes ever to be tried in this courtroom. How do you plead?'

The public gallery was packed and the jury was staring at me accusingly. My mouth felt like a sandpit in the Simpson Desert.

'Not guilty,' I croaked. 'I'm innocent. I didn't do it. Honest.'

The prosecutor was on her feet. 'I put it to you,' she said, 'that on fourteenth of November last, at bed-time, you read your children *The Twits* by Roald Dahl and that you wilfully and intentionally left out the bit about the wormy spaghetti because you didn't want to miss the start of the footy on telly.'

'Not true,' I cried. 'It wasn't footy, it was netball.'

The jury stared at me without blinking. Stuffed toys can be very stern.

I put my head in my hands.

'All right,' I moaned, 'I admit it. I couldn't bear to read all of *The Twits* again. I'd read it 127 times in the past year.'

My son took the witness stand.

'That wasn't the worst example,' he said to the prosecutor. 'In July, Dad read us *War and Peace* and all we got was, "Once upon a time there was a war, and then there was peace, the end."'

'I couldn't stand it again,' I moaned. 'Not for the eleventh time.'

'And was that,' said the prosecutor to her brother, 'the same week he read us "Ode to a Nightingale" by the very famous English poet John Keats?'

Dylan looked at her sadly. 'He said it was Keats, but we just didn't think that "Tweet, tweet, OK kids, time to settle down now, *The Bill*'s started" sounded much like a classic poem.'

It was a long trial.

I was found guilty.

When the main witness for the prosecution

returned to his judge's chair and put his fluffy toilet-seat cover wig back on, I looked pleadingly at the jury for mercy.

Nothing.

The jury foreman, who'd just taken her prosecutor's dressing gown off, explained to me that the jury were pushing for a long sentence, except for one of the fluffy pink teddies, who wanted death.

Fortunately the judge didn't agree.

He sentenced me to nineteen years hard labour.

I knew what that meant.

I groaned and reached for *The Twits*.

Sunday, 24 January

I've always encouraged the kids to stand up for what they know is right, and I'm pleased to say I think I've succeeded.

Take today for example.

'We want you to promise,' the kids said to me this morning, 'to look after our polluted planet and not make any more unnecessary trips in the car.'

'I promise,' I said.

They opened the boot and let me out.

'Because let's face it, Dad,' said Maddy, 'you are very lazy when it comes to walking.'

'Not any more,' I protested. 'This week I did the supermarket shopping on foot.'

'Only partly,' said Dylan. 'You got exhausted between Frozen Foods and Breakfast Cereals and hitched a ride on someone's trolley.'

Kids, they don't miss anything.

'OK,' I said. 'But on Friday I went to the dentist on foot.'

'Part of the way,' said Maddy. 'We had to carry you the last fifty metres as usual.'

I sighed. And then gasped when the kids said they wanted us to do our trip to the museum today by public transport.

'By leaving the car at home and taking the train,' said Maddy, 'we'll be reducing our consumption of scarce fossil fuels and our emission of harmful gases.'

I think that's what she said. I'd locked myself in the car after the word 'train'.

'It's not a long drive,' I mouthed through the window. 'Just a couple of litres of unleaded.'

Using hand signals and the karaoke amplifier,

the kids reminded me about our previous car trip to the city. After driving there (2.3 litres), we'd looked for a parking spot (19.7 litres). Failing to find one, we'd parked on the footpath (8.6 litres – it was a high kerb). We'd returned from the museum to find a parking ticket on the car (5.2 litres attending court to dispute the fine, 164 litres getting the car back from Bundaberg after it was stolen from outside the courtroom).

The kids had made their point.

We were on the platform in plenty of time for the 12.15 train to the city. So were lots of other families with stubborn kids like mine.

A metallic voice crackled above us.

'The 12.15 train to the city is running eighty-seven minutes late due to running into the back of the 11.47 which was running thirty-one minutes late due to the driver being late to work due to the trains running late.'

I took a deep breath.

Boy, it's not easy treating our planet with care and respect. I still haven't forgotten the fiasco with our new solar hot-water system. I mean, where in the owner's manual does it say, 'Don't put block-out cream on the solar panels'?

On the platform the kids made a pensioner squeeze up so I could sit down.

'Try and relax, Dad,' they said. 'Getting angry and breathing heavily increases your carbon dioxide output and contributes to global warming.'

The 11.28 arrived soon after one o'clock and we travelled into town.

At the museum there was an old train on display. I asked the staff if it could be returned to service, possibly at 12.15 each day. They explained it was too old. They said they were, however, expecting a newer train which had been donated last year but which was running thirty-seven weeks late.

When we arrived at the city station for the trip home, the platform was packed. The train arrived on time. Applause broke out. The kids told me to stop as I was the only one doing it.

'See?' they said. 'Public transport isn't so bad.'

Then we noticed that the train had only half the usual number of carriages.

'We always run smaller trains on the weekend,'

said a railway employee as he disappeared under the surging mob.

We were packed in like sardines in a really small bit of ocean.

The kids didn't seem to mind, but I was thin-lipped the entire trip home. I tried not to be, but I had someone's umbrella hooked into one corner of my mouth and someone else's two year old hooked into the other.

We managed to struggle off the train three stops past ours. We made it back to the station carpark before midnight. The car had been stolen.

I'm writing this while I wait for the train to Bundaberg.

It's running thirty-eight minutes late.

Luckily the kids aren't here to check my breathing.

My Problem Is I Don't Know When To Stop

'Oh Graham, pet,' said Mrs Glossop, looking upset, 'this sentence is so long,' and it's true I've only got myself to blame, I did completely ignore an instruction from a teacher because as Mrs Glossop says herself, 'full stops are our friends and we must learn how to use them,' but I ignored her in English on account of when I pick up a pen and use my imagination I don't want it to stop, so Mrs Glossop sentenced me to a week of lunchtime detention which wasn't that long really, not given I'd be completely finished now if I hadn't asked for another twenty-seven offences to be taken into consideration including skipping the full stops when I read a book and scratching my initials onto Anthony Webster's lunch box without any full stops and scribbling out all the full stops in all the books in the public library which was clearly an exaggeration (so was the lunch box) but on my last day of lunchtime detention two detectives arrived at school and asked me lots of questions in a very hot room about vandalism in libraries and completely ignored me when I reminded them that I'm a very keen reader and I've had my own library card since I was three, not to mention my own lunch box since I was four, facts they ignored because they were too busy growling at me about criminal behaviour and getting me convicted and sentenced to ninety-nine years which made Mrs Glossop burst into tears when she came to visit me here in my cell and carry on about how my sentence is so terribly long except I have to say there was something completely fake about her tears and she had a look in her eyes which has left me very suspicious that the reason I'm locked up in this high-security boys home isn't because of any scribbled library books or scratched lunch boxes, it's because I gave Mrs Glossop a very long sentence and now she's given me one back.

Imagine That

Before we set off, I check the air in the tyres.

An angry voice yells at me.

'Oi, what do you think you're doing?'

I look round, surprised. Isn't it obvious?

'It's going to be a long trip,' I say, 'so I'm checking the air in the tyres.'

The airport official gives me a very stern look and takes away my tyre-pressure gauge.

'I think, young man,' he says, 'you'd better go back inside the terminal. Touching the planes is a criminal offence.'

I tell him I'm sorry, but I'm concerned about airline safety. Particularly the dangers of cornering fast on a wet runway with under-inflated tyres.

The official sighs.

'All the tyres on all the planes are checked regularly,' he says.

'What about the shock absorbers?' I ask.

'The shock absorbers too,' he says.

I tell him I hope so. I remind him that shock absorbers are tricky things that can go bung at any time, for example backing over a speed bump in the supermarket carpark or landing at Cairns. Specially if there are speed bumps on the runway.

'Can I climb onto a wing and jump up and down a bit?' I ask the official. 'Just to be sure.'

He has me escorted to the terminal by anti-terrorist commandos.

They take me to an interrogation room.

'How did you do it?' demands the airport security supervisor. 'How did you manage to get past airport security and onto the tarmac?'

'I hid in a suitcase,' I explain. 'I saw a lady checking she'd remembered to bring spare underwear, then she forgot to lock her case. So I hopped in. It was a tight squeeze, but Mum once showed me a yoga position where you put your feet over your shoulders.'

The interrogation room goes silent.

All the security officers are staring at me.

I know why.

'The lady had remembered to put her jogging shoes in her case as well,' I say. 'That's why I've got these tread marks on my forehead.'

The security officers look at each other. I can see they're making a mental note to keep a special eye out in future for suitcases with ladies' underwear and jogging shoes and eleven-year-old boys in them.

'Why?' says the airport security supervisor. 'Why did you do it?'

'Wouldn't you?' I say. 'Wouldn't you do a safety check if you and the family you love were about to be taken six thousand metres up in the air without a ladder or a parachute or a big pile of fluffy cushions?'

'Sorry about that,' murmurs Dad when the airport security people finally find him browsing in the airport bookshop. 'I'm afraid our Garth gets a bit carried away sometimes.'

'We think Garth's amazing, actually,' says Mum, strolling over from the other side of the shop and giving me a hug. 'He's got an incredible imagination.'

'No, he hasn't,' says my little brother Amon. 'He's just scared of flying.'

'I'm not,' I explain to the airport security people. 'I just believe in exercising the same care and caution with planes as I do with everything else. I check cutlery for metal fatigue. I examine sandwiches for leaks. I test Amon for loose teeth. Why not planes?'

'See?' says Mum to the airport security people. 'So imaginative.'

'Last time we were at the airport,' chuckles Dad, 'he took all the wheels off a 747 to check the brake pads and we were only there to meet someone.'

'Leave him with us,' says Mum. 'We'll keep an eye on him.'

Before the airport security people can reply, or put handcuffs on me, a senior flight captain runs into the bookshop.

'Arrest that boy,' he says.

I brace myself. I know why the captain is looking so annoyed.

'This child,' says the captain, 'has been in the air-crew locker room upsetting the pilots.'

'I didn't mean to upset them,' I protest. 'I was just checking they were OK to fly.'

Everyone is looking at me now, even the other customers in the airport bookshop.

'He tried to shine a torch up their bottoms,' says the captain accusingly.

'It was a medical check,' I explain. 'If a pilot's kidneys become inflamed at six thousand metres, it could jeopardise the safety of everyone on board.'

The airport security people make Dad sign a document promising I'll behave myself on the flight. I want to read it first in case there are big fines involved, or spelling mistakes, but the airport security supervisor is making impatient gestures with his metal-detection wand.

'Can I have my tyre-pressure gauge and torch back, please?' I say to him.

He thinks about this.

'I'll have to disable them first,' he says.

He takes the batteries out of the torch. He looks for

batteries in the tyre-pressure gauge. There aren't any. So he snaps off the little metal rod that tells you the tyre pressures.

'Sorry,' he says as he hands them to me, but he doesn't look very sorry.

The airport security people march me and Mum and Dad and Amon onto the plane ages before any of the other passengers.

Is it, I wonder, so we'll have time to check the internal wiring?

I decide it probably isn't.

The security people sit me in my seat, click my seatbelt, and lock it using a secret lock. Which is good. I once read online how a plane hit an air pocket over Uzbekistan and plummeted two thousand metres in six seconds and the seatbelt of a 37-year-old man popped open completely of its own accord. After the plane had landed, luckily, but still.

The wait for take-off isn't easy.

Wobbly thoughts buzz around in my head like an airbus with a faulty entertainment system and no reading lights and only one wing.

Have they greased the handbrake cable on both sides? I wonder. Will they remember to replace the fuel cap? Which is our nearest exit? How can I be sure without a tape measure?

Suddenly we're moving, rolling backwards, and then speeding down the runway with no time to inspect the life jackets for dry-cleaning damage or blow into the oxygen mask to dislodge any airline food that might be blocking the tube.

Before I can ask a flight attendant to bring me an emergency dinghy and inflate it so I can see how it's done, there's a roar and everything shudders, and I'm pressed back into my seat, and not by a flight attendant.

Suddenly we're up in the air.

I sit there, keeping my eyes closed for a long time. A very long time.

Then I remove the in-flight magazine from between my teeth and say a silent prayer of thanks that somebody has obviously remembered to check the fanbelt.

I glance across the aisle at Mum and Dad, who are both calmly reading. Next to me, Amon is folding his air-safety card into a fighter plane.

All around us, other passengers are looking just as relaxed.

I take a few deep breaths. Actually, this isn't so bad. I'm starting to feel sort of relaxed too.

I unclick my seatbelt and lean forward and slide my backpack out from under the seat in front. I pull the book Dad bought me out of the seat pocket and put it away in the backpack. I check that my wallet is in there too. It is, with all my holiday money in it. I'm glad I didn't waste my savings buying a torch or a tyre-pressure gauge.

It's a brilliant book, Overcoming Your Fear of Flying, specially the chapter about using your imagination to distract yourself in the minutes leading up to take-off. But I won't be needing the book any more, because it worked.

Here I am, my first time up in a plane, six thousand metres in the air without a ladder or a parachute or a big pile of fluffy cushions, sitting here with my eyes wide open, and suddenly I'm not scared of flying at all.

Imagine that.

Big Mistake

It all started with bosoms.

When me and Imelda were babies, Mum used to breastfeed us. Those were the happiest meals I've ever had, even better than spicy sausage pizza. Until Imelda spoiled everything.

Even nine years later I can still remember what happened. Me sucking away happily on Mum's left side as usual. Imelda doing the same on the other side. Until suddenly Imelda stopped sucking and glared at me across the valley.

'Donald's bosom is bigger than mine,' she wailed.

Mum didn't know what Imelda's wail meant, of course. But I understood. And it was totally ridiculous.

No way was the bosom in my mouth bigger than the one in Imelda's.

'No, it's not,' I wailed. 'Hers is bigger.'

I'd never compared Mum's bosoms before, but as soon as Imelda got pushy I could clearly see that my bosom was actually smaller than Imelda's bosom.

'Not fair,' I wailed. 'Hers is much bigger.'

'Rubbish,' wailed Imelda. 'His is.'

Mum didn't have a clue what we were on about. But she could see we weren't happy, so she burped us and checked our nappies for recent visitors and tickled us under our chins and got us sucking again.

Imelda didn't make any more wild accusations that day. Or that year. But every mealtime as she sucked grumpily and glared at me from her side I could see what she was thinking.

His is bigger.

I glared back.

I was thinking the same thing.

Hers is bigger.

When you're a twin it's very important that the other twin doesn't get more than you. You probably have to be a twin to understand how important that is. How very very important.

I knew it wasn't going to end with bosoms.

It didn't.

On our first birthday Dad made us a cake in the shape of Thomas the Tank Engine. Me and Imelda both loved Thomas, so we were very happy.

At first.

All our aunties and uncles and grandparents were there and they helped us blow out the candles. We had one candle each. Exactly the same size. I checked and Imelda did too.

Mum cut the cake and gave us half a Fat Controller each.

Imelda's face went red with distress. She pointed at my plate and said her first word.

'Bigger.'

Mum had cut the Fat Controller so we each had one side of his body, including half his bottom. Imelda was saying that my Fat Controller buttock was bigger than her Fat Controller buttock.

Which was rubbish.

I pointed at Imelda's plate and said my first two words.

'Bigger buttock.'

We both burst into tears.

All the grown-ups tried to make our birthday happy again. Mum offered us exactly half a coal truck each instead, then realised that one of the coal truck's eyebrows was bigger than the other. Auntie Pauline explained how most people in real life don't have perfectly matching buttocks, and pointed to Uncle John's. Dad got a bowl of icing and added an extra pair of underpants to each half of the Fat Controller's bottom to try and disguise their size, but me and Imelda saw through that.

Poor Mum and Dad.

Every birthday it was the same.

When we were five, me and Imelda both asked for exactly the same birthday present. A tape measure. Mum and Dad gave us one each.

Identical tape measures.

Or so they thought.

Imelda measured my tape measure with hers, and I measured hers with mine, and soon we were both in tears.

'His is .06 of a millimetre longer,' sobbed Imelda.

'Hers is .0003 of a millimetre thicker,' I wailed. 'And her wrapping paper is wider too.'

When we started school, they put Imelda in one class and me in another. It didn't work.

'His teacher is bigger than mine,' wailed Imelda. 'I measured them.'

Every day it was the same.

'His fish fingers are bigger than mine,' sobbed Imelda one evening.

'Hers are,' I wailed.

'They can't be,' shouted Mum. 'They're made in a factory. With millions of dollars worth of equipment scientifically designed to make sure every fish finger is exactly the same size as every other fish finger. That's why we have fish fingers four times a week.'

Imelda and me thought about this.

'It's the way you cook them,' wailed Imelda. 'You make mine shrink.'

'Mine shrink more,' I sobbed.

Mum grabbed our plates and dumped the fish fingers onto the chopping board.

'Right,' she said. 'Here's what we're going to do. You're each going to cut your fish fingers exactly in half. I suggest you use your tape measures. Then you're each going to choose which halves you want, one piece at a time, taking it in turns, so you both end up with exactly the same number of halves, which each of you will have chosen yourself.'

Mum gave a weary sigh.

'Let's see you find a reason for squabbling then,' she said. 'I should have thought of this years ago.'

Mum handed us a knife each.

Me and Imelda grabbed our tape measures, and measured the knives.

'His is bigger than mine,' sobbed Imelda.

'Hers is,' I wailed.

The years passed. Nothing changed. Except Mum and Dad got wearier. Sometimes I felt guilty, but I couldn't stop. I couldn't give in. I couldn't let Imelda get more than me. You can't do that, not when you're a twin.

Whenever I thought about the future, I realised life would always be the same in our family. Until Mum and Dad got so old and weary, they died. And the undertaker sent us their ashes and Imelda reckoned I'd got a bigger share and I reckoned she had.

That was our future.

Until last week, when we went on holiday.

I think it was the motel muesli that was the last straw. ('He's got bigger bran flakes than me.' 'She's got bigger particles of hydrogenated kelp.')

Or maybe the last straw was in the service station. ('She's got a bigger straw than me.' 'His 275-ml carton of chocolate milk is bigger than my 275-ml carton of chocolate milk.')

Or maybe it was the drive up the coast. ('He spilt more chocolate milk on the car seat than I did.' 'She did a bigger sick in the glove box than I did.')

Whichever it was, at lunchtime everything changed.

We were having a picnic in a park near the highway. Sandwiches ('hers is crustier') and bananas ('his is more bent').

'For the love of Pete,' said Dad wearily. 'When are you two going to grow up and stop whingeing and whining?'

I looked around at the other families having picnics. Happy laughing families with kids who weren't squabbling and parents who weren't weary and miserable.

I looked at their cars. None of them had luggage on the roof like ours. Probably because their boots weren't full of tape measures and rulers and microscopes and weighing scales and surveyor's tripods and portable laser measuring devices.

Suddenly I felt weary and miserable too.

I wanted our family to be one of the happy ones.

We'd eaten most of our picnic. There were just two bananas left. You didn't need a measuring device to see that one was big and one was small.

Mum and Dad were pretending those bananas didn't exist. I could see they were hoping me and Imelda would do the same.

I picked up the big one and held it out to Imelda.

'Here,' I said. 'You have it.'

Imelda stared at me, stunned. So did Mum and Dad.

'You want me to have the big banana?' said Imelda, amazed.

I nodded.

I could see Imelda's mind working fast. Her eyes narrowed. I could see she was looking for the catch.

Then she grinned.

'No thanks,' she said. 'I don't need it.'

I was confused. Was she saying she wanted me to have it?

Before I could decide, Imelda jumped up, grabbed hold of my hand and dragged me round the other side of some bushes.

'I don't need your banana,' she said sweetly, 'because I've got a bigger banana than you'll ever have.'

I stared.

In front of us was a gigantic banana. It must have been at least 30 metres long. And three times as tall as a grown-up. It looked like it was made of plastic. On the side of it was a sign.

The Big Banana, Coffs Harbour, NSW.

'I win,' said Imelda.

For a moment I hoped this was just a game, that we were having fun like the other families. But Imelda was looking at me in a very mocking way and I could see from her eyes that she was deadly serious.

I realised what had happened.

Imelda had listened to Dad and decided that now we were ten, we were too old for whingeing and whining. She'd decided that now we were old enough for gloating and winning.

Everything had changed, and nothing had.

She'd won with the banana. I knew there couldn't be a bigger banana anywhere in Australia. But that was only Round One.

Later that afternoon, further up the highway, we passed The Big Prawn and I spotted it first which made it mine.

'I've got a bigger prawn than you,' I gloated to Imelda.

She seethed.

In the front of the car, Mum and Dad, who'd been feeling a bit light-headed from three whole hours without any whingeing and whining, sagged into their seats.

The rest of the week was a nightmare.

As we toured around on our driving holiday, me and Imelda couldn't relax for a second. We hardly dared blink in case we missed something.

I got The Big Peanut, The Big Crab and I was in the middle of gloating to Imelda that I had a bigger bottom than her when Mum wearily pointed out that what I'd just seen wasn't The Big Buttock, it was a haystack covered with pink plastic.

Imelda got The Big Pineapple, The Big Cow and what she claimed was The Big Swimming Pool, which it wasn't because it was the same size as a normal swimming pool, just on its side.

'Cheat,' I sneered at her.

'Jealous,' she sneered back.

'Please,' sighed Mum wearily.

We'd never been more unhappy.

I started imagining big things and desperately hoping they'd be round the next corner so I could see them first and win.

The Big Flyscreen.

The Big Teabag.

The Big Blood Clot if we passed an abattoir.

Nothing.

Dad started going out of his way to avoid big things. He saw in a tourist brochure that the next town had The Big Tow Truck, so he took a dirt track through a swamp to keep us away from it.

We got bogged in the mud.

While Mum and Dad tried to get us out, me and Imelda gathered dry grass and branches on the higher ground to put under the back wheels. Except Imelda wasn't doing much gathering. She was too busy gloating.

'I've got bigger bosoms than you,' she said in a very cocky voice.

I looked up.

Imelda was sneering at me across the little valley we were in and pointing towards the horizon. In the distance, next to what must have been the highway, was a huge advertising billboard with an ad for a caravan park. Most of it was a woman with half her bosoms showing.

I stared at it for a long time.

Imelda kept on gloating for a long time.

I didn't care. I was thinking about a long time ago, when all this had started. When Imelda reckoned I had the biggest bosom and I reckoned she had.

We couldn't both have been right. Then another thought hit me. What if we'd both been wrong? What if Mum's bosoms were exactly the same size? All this whingeing and whining and gloating and winning wouldn't be necessary anymore.

Suddenly I wanted to know the truth.

That night, in the motel, I took a peek.

Mum was having a shower. Dad and Imelda were watching a movie on TV. During an exciting bit when they were totally engrossed, I crept over to the bathroom, opened the door and peeped in.

Just as I did, the shower screen slid open and Mum stepped out.

She saw me looking.

'Oh for Pete's sake,' she said, grabbing a towel and wrapping it around herself. 'Can't a person get a moment's peace in this family?'

My guts went tight and cold. Not because Mum was annoyed. Because of what I'd seen.

Mum's left bosom was slightly bigger than her right one. And it hung slightly lower. Which made it seem even larger.

'What's wrong, love?' said Mum

She must have noticed my miserable face.

'Imelda was right,' I said sadly.

'Right about what?' said Mum.

'That my bosom was bigger than hers,' I said.

'Of course I was right,' said Imelda, coming over. She gave me a jealous look. 'Your bosom was always bigger.'

Mum frowned and looked puzzled. Then she grinned.

'What a pair of nongs,' she said.

For a moment I thought she was talking about her bosoms. But she wasn't, she was talking about me and Imelda.

'You didn't have a bosom each,' said Mum. 'You couldn't. The right-hand one didn't feed properly. The milk kept getting blocked. So I fed you both with the left one, taking turns.'

I stared at her.

'But I can remember us both sucking at once,' I said. 'I can remember it.'

'So can I,' said Imelda.

Mum shook her head.

'Nope,' she said.

'Wasn't possible,' said Dad, who had come over to us.

'When we get home,' said Mum, 'I'll show you the doctor's report from the baby health centre. I was a lefty. That's why it sags a bit now.'

I looked at Imelda. I could see she was as shocked as I was.

'The right one was a waiting and burping area,' said Mum. 'While one of you was feeding on the left side, I'd cuddle the other one of you on the right side.'

Me and Imelda stood there for a long time, just staring at Mum's towel-covered chest.

Mum let us. I think she could see that me and Imelda had some important things to think about.

'Don't you mind,' I said to Mum after a while, 'That we made one a bit saggy?'

'Course not,' said Mum. 'It's what it's for. Anyway, when I've got a pair of anything, I always like them both exactly the same amount.'

Dad nodded.

Mum gave me and Imelda a long look.

I realised she wasn't just talking about her bosoms.

I glanced over and saw that Imelda had realised this too, and was feeling as good about it as I was.

Imelda opened her mouth to say something. I wondered if she was going to boast about having a worse memory than me.

For a moment I wanted to be the one to boast about having the worst memory.

But I didn't.

I decided to give Imelda the chance.

Imelda stayed silent.

After a while I realised she was giving me the chance.

We swapped a little grin. Mum gave us both a hug. And then there was no need for me or Imelda to say anything.

Odd Socques

Macques was dreading the spelling test.

The minute he walked into class and saw the substitute teacher sitting at Ms Conway's desk, he knew there'd be one.

Substitute teachers always did spelling tests.

'Good morning 6C,' said the substitute teacher. 'Ms Conway is away today. My name's Mr Green.'

Macques could see something bulging in Mr Green's jacket pocket.

Spelling test prizes.

'Good morning, Mr Green,' chanted the class.

'OK 6C,' said Mr Green. 'I've heard you're very good at maths and spelling. Would you rather have a maths test or a spelling test?'

Macques sighed gloomily.

He knew exactly what was coming.

'Spelling,' yelled the class.

Mr Green looked around at all the shining eyes and excited faces. He allowed himself a quiet smile.

A spelling class.

He'd spotted it the minute they walked in.

Then Mr Green spotted something else. A boy up the back, a boy with brown hair and a sad face, who didn't seem very delighted at all.

Can't be helped, thought Mr Green. Every class has at least one bad speller.

He pulled the bag of mini chocolate bars from his jacket pocket and waited for the cheer a teacher with lollies always got.

It didn't happen.

Mr Green looked around the class, surprised.

'A mini chocolate bar for every word you get right,' he said, in case this lot were a bit slow and didn't get how substitute teacher spelling tests worked.

Still no cheer.

Mr Green felt a moment of panic.

But only a moment. The class were still looking excited and enthusiastic. Eyes still gleaming and lots of smiles. Except the boy up the back.

How unusual, thought Mr Green. This lot seem to like spelling tests more than they like lollies.

He decided to keep the words simple, in case he was right the first time and they were a bit slow.

'OK,' he said. 'First word. Pivot. Hands up.'

Hands shot up.

Mr Green chose a girl at the front.

'P-I-V-O-T,' said Jane Dillon.

'Good,' said Mr Green and tossed her a chocolate. 'Next word, diesel.'

Sam Webster got it right.

Over the next few minutes the class also got snail, patch, gravity, blood, digital, drought, tickle and splash.

Macques wasn't surprised. He knew from experience the class were good spellers.

They'll probably get every single one, he thought gloomily. Until Mr Green asks them the one they're waiting for.

Which, a few minutes later, Mr Green did.

'Fax,' he said, taking another mini chocolate bar from the bag. 'Listen carefully. Not facts, fax.'

Every hand in the room shot up. Except Macques's.

Mr Green pointed to Tina Walsh.

'F-A-C-Q-U-E-S,' said Tina.

Mr Green looked at her, his hand frozen in mid-toss, the mini chocolate bar still between his fingers.

Strange, he thought. I wasn't told about any special needs students in this class. Perhaps she's just a comedian.

He gave her a quick frown, then pointed to the boy next to her.

'You have a go,' he said. 'Fax.'

'F-A-C-Q-U-E-S,' said Garth Spence.

Mr Green felt his face going hot.

OK, he knew what this was. Not a spelling test. A substitute teacher test.

Mr Green took a deep breath. He prided himself on always passing such tests. Well, almost always. There was the one unfortunate incident when he'd shouted at a boy for several minutes from a distance of about three centimetres, but that was months ago.

Mr Green unwrapped the untossed chocolate bar,

popped it into his mouth and savoured it like he was at a wine tasting.

This didn't get the laugh he'd hoped for, but at least he was showing them he was in control.

'Let me help you,' he said to the class. 'Here's another word very similar to fax. Sax. It's short for saxophone, my favourite musical instrument. Any jazz fans here?'

Everybody put their hands up, except the sad boy.

Mr Green had a feeling this class probably weren't jazz fans, but he pressed on.

'You,' he said, pointing to a girl. 'The word is sax.'

'S-A-C-Q-U-E-S,' said Lilly Potter.

Mr Green hesitated, not sure what to do next.

Move on to 'tax', or a maths test?

'Sir,' said a boy at the front. 'There is one person in the class who might know. His name is . . .'

The boy was trying not to giggle and he spluttered the name as he said it, but Mr Green was pretty sure it was 'Max'.

Mr Green smiled to himself. Perhaps this was a trap, perhaps it wasn't. Either way he'd win. Always easier to punish one ringleader than a whole class.

'Thank you,' he said to the boy at the front. 'Max, where are you? Stand up please.'

Slowly Macques stood up.

He didn't try to explain. He'd tried with too many other substitute teachers and he always got the blame anyway.

He knew the rest of the class were watching him. He knew they were struggling not to laugh. They always preferred to do their laughing a bit later, after the substitute teacher had got angry.

'Max,' said Mr Green. 'Spell your name for us please.'

'M-A-C-Q-U-E-S,' said Macques, wishing for the millionth time in his life that his parents hadn't done this to him.

As usual, Macques walked home from school on his own.

Near the corner of his street he heard somebody running up behind him.

Macques told himself to relax. He reminded himself that the bullying almost never happened this close to the house. But when he turned to see who it was, he still felt a jolt of anxiety.

It was Sam Webster.

'That sucked,' said Sam. 'When that substitute teacher yelled at you. Unfair.'

Macques glanced nervously up and down the street. Sam Webster usually hung out in a gang and he didn't usually have anything to say to Macques. So why was he here now?

Macques could only think of one reason. The street sign a couple of metres away. The one showing the name of Macques's street.

Knocques Avenue.

Macques glared up at the sign like he did every afternoon. He wished he could rip it down. If only someone had done that ages ago, before its stupid spelling had inspired Mum and Dad when they were looking for baby name ideas.

But it was still there and now it was the perfect mocking spot.

Max braced himself for a mocking.

Then he saw that Sam was glancing nervously up and down the street too.

'Can you keep a secret?' muttered Sam.

Macques peered around again. He couldn't see

anyone else from school lurking about. He hesitated for a moment, wondering if Sam was for real. Could you trust a kid who flicked snot at substitute teachers behind their backs?

There was a kind of haunted look on Sam's face that made Macques want to trust him.

'Yes,' said Macques quietly. 'I can keep a secret.'

'Let's keep walking,' said Sam. 'I don't want anybody to hear this.'

They walked along Macques's street.

Macques waited for Sam to speak.

Sam looked as though he was having some sort of pain, possibly in the guts. Macques wondered if Sam had an allergy to mini chocolate bars.

Poor bloke, he thought, that'd be a bit rough.

Finally Sam spoke.

'I've got a dumb name too,' he muttered.

Macques looked at Sam, surprised.

Sam wasn't a silly name, nor was Webster, so it must be a secret middle one. Parents did all sorts of bad things with middle names. The worst ones were usually from dead pop singers or footy players. Elvis and Archibald, stuff like that.

Macques waited for Sam to unburden himself.

'Sam isn't spelt S-A-M,' said Sam, staring at the footpath. 'It's spelt S-A-H-M.'

Macques looked at him, even more surprised.

'My parents didn't want me to have an ordinary name,' said Sahm gloomily. 'They wanted me to be special and different and um, what's that other thing, unique.'

Macques knew all about parents wanting that.

'But . . .' said Macques. 'How did you . . . I mean how come nobody knows? How come you don't get the same treatment as me?'

Sahm glanced up and down the street again.

'I was lucky,' he said. 'When I enrolled in school the office got it wrong. They thought S-A-H-M was a spelling mistake, so they put me down as S-A-M. My parents never found out. Nor did the other kids. But next year we go to high school. Nobody gets that lucky twice in a row. What can I do?'

Macques thought about this.

'How come your parents haven't spotted that the school is spelling your name wrong?' he asked. 'The school sends letters home all the time.'

Sahm didn't seem to hear the question.

Macques wasn't surprised.

Sahm's face was desperate and pleading. Obviously all he could think about was avoiding six years of high school bullying and misery.

Macques knew exactly how Sahm felt.

For a few seconds Macques hesitated.

Should he tell Sahm his secret? It was risky. He hadn't told anybody his confidential plan to survive high school. If it got into the wrong hands, the whole thing would be ruined and the next six years would be as bad as the last six had been.

But Sahm needed his help.

'Listen,' said Macques quietly. 'I've been talking on a chat site to some other kids with tragic names like ours. They reckon they know people who can hack into any school computer in Australia. These people charge a lot, but I'm saving up. Once I've enrolled in high school, I'm going to chuck my student card away, pay them to hack in and change my name to the proper spelling, then get a replacement card.'

Macques realised he was out of breath, even though he and Sahm had reached Macques's front gate and had stopped walking.

Sahm's eyes were shining.

'It's two hundred dollars,' said Macques. 'Can you save that much?'

Sahm didn't reply. He stuck his hands into his pockets.

'If they do yours at the same time as mine,' said Macques, 'perhaps I can get them to charge you a cheaper price.'

Sahm still didn't say anything.

Macques understood. Sahm was probably in shock about how expensive a safe and happy high school education was these days. Macques was feeling very stressed himself. If any of the kids at school found out about this . . .

Suddenly Sahm gave a big relieved grin.

'Thanks,' he said, and slapped Macques on the back.

'Think about it,' said Macques. 'If you want to give it a go, let me know.'

'I will,' said Sahm. 'Thank you so much. You're a legend.'

For a second Macques thought his new friend was going to burst into tears. Sam was struggling to keep his face under control.

Poor bloke, thought Macques. I won't invite him in. Give him a bit of time on his own to calm himself down.

He gave Sahm a wave and headed for the front door.

On his way there, he had a nagging thought. The way Sahm had slapped him on the back. Kids at school didn't usually do that. Not unless . . .

At the front door Macques turned and glanced back at Sahm. And saw the giggling faces of the rest of the gang, crouching in the hedge.

Sahm, or rather Sam, didn't look tearful any more. He was laughing even harder than the others.

Macques managed to get the key in the lock. Inside, once the door was shut, he squeezed his eyes closed and struggled with his own tears.

Real ones.

Then he wiped his eyes and checked his back in the hall mirror. He wasn't surprised to see something stuck there.

A yellow post-it note with two words scrawled on it.

Tricqued You.

Macques waited until dinner time to have another go at Mum and Dad.

'Please let me change my name,' he begged. 'Please let me spell it M-A-X.'

Mum and Dad looked at each other.

They both sighed, but they didn't say anything until they'd finished chewing their mouthfuls of pan-seared swordfish with balsamic vinegar and pink peppercorns.

'Darling,' said Mum. 'We've explained this to you so often. Macques is a lovely name. It's special and distinctive and unique. Like you.'

'Forget those pea-brains at school,' said Dad. 'Once you're out in the big wide world, you'll be glad you've got a name that people notice. In those hospitals or TV stations or nuclear research facilities or wherever you end up working, there'll be all the ordinary Maxes, but only one Macques.'

Mum and Dad both glowed.

Macques wasn't sure if it was from pride or pink peppercorns.

'I want to be an ordinary Max,' he said.

This time Mum and Dad didn't wait till they'd finished chewing.

'That is crazy talk,' said Mum. 'You are not ordinary.'

'I am,' said Macques.

'Rubbish,' said Dad. 'When you were born we decided we weren't going to let you be ordinary. That's why we didn't give you a boring ordinary name like our parents gave us.'

'Eric and Joan are nice names,' said Macques.

Mum and Dad both sighed crossly.

'When will you get it into your head?' said Dad. 'You won't stand out in the crowd if people think you're ordinary and boring.'

'Why do you think me and Dad go to so much trouble?' said Mum.

Macques knew what was coming next.

Mum swung her feet out from under the table, pulled up the legs of her black tracksuit and pointed to her socks. One was pink, one was orange.

'I'm the only person at the gym with odd socks,' she said. 'Nobody there thinks I'm ordinary.'

Dad twanged his braces. They had green sheep on them.

'One look at my braces,' said Dad, 'and everyone in my office knows I'm not ordinary.'

'Do you see, Macques?' said Mum. 'Do you see what we're saying?'

Macques replied through gritted teeth.

'Yes,' he said. 'You're saying that the reason you drive the same foreign cars as everyone else and wear the same designer clothes as everyone else and eat the same swordfish with balsamic vinegar and pink peppercorns as everyone else is so everyone will think you're not ordinary.'

'Macques,' said Mum.

'Careful, young man,' said Dad.

'But you are ordinary,' said Macques. 'I am too.'

Macques realised he was standing up and shouting and several of his pink peppercorns were on the handwoven Icelandic tablecloth.

He didn't care.

'I just want us to be an ordinary family,' he pleaded.

'Macques,' yelled Mum. 'Stop yelling. We do not yell in this house.'

'Go to your room,' said Dad with icy calm. 'Have a long hard think. I don't want to see you or hear a peep from you until you come to your senses.'

'Nor do I,' said Mum.

Macques threw himself onto his bed and buried his face in his Scandinavian-style organic goose-down pillow.

I can't take it any more, he thought desperately.

He used to think he could.

He used to think that if he got through life one day at a time, he could make it to his eighteenth birthday and then leave home and change his name.

Not any more.

'Help,' he whispered into his pillow. 'I need help.'

Then he stopped. One thing he'd learned in life was that pillows couldn't help with the really big problems. Small ones, like being tired or having a stiff neck, yes. Big ones, like war and disease and having a stupid name, no.

The other reason Macques stopped was that somebody was tapping at his window.

He jumped up.

Even before he opened the curtain, Macques felt anger burning through him.

Sam Webster and his gang. Still loitering in the front yard. Still hoping to get a bit more taunting and mocking in before bedtime.

Thank you Sam, thought Macques grimly. You don't know it, but I'm very glad you're still here. When I haul you in through that window and drag you down to Mum and Dad, then maybe they'll understand.

Macques flung the curtains open.

And stared.

It wasn't Sam and his mates.

Four other kids were standing outside looking at Macques through the glass. It was dark out there, but the light from the room shone on their faces. Two boys and two girls, all wearing white overalls. Macques had never seen any of them before.

One of the boys signalled to Macques to open the window.

Macques hesitated. Then he saw that the boy had a name tag on his overalls. It said *Nickless*.

Max opened the window.

'G'day,' said the boy. 'Unfair Name Rescue Squad. Are you Macques spelled M-A-C-Q-U-E-S?'

Dazed, Macques nodded.

'We're here to rescue you,' said the boy.

Macques didn't understand.

He saw that the others had name tags too. The other boy's said Shorn. The girls' were Jeen and Kaitye.

'Sorry we've taken a while to get to you,' said Jeen. 'Big backlog.'

'Unfair Name Rescue Squad?' said Macques.

Then he realised what was going on. It was another trick. The most complicated piece of bullying and mockery yet. These kids weren't even from his school. Somebody must have paid them.

'Do you want to be rescued?' said Kaitye.

Macques nodded.

He could see they'd even got a taxi waiting out in the street. It was perfect. He'd pretend to go along with them, and when they all got to the taxi he'd yell for Mum and Dad. Then Mum and Dad would see the sort of thing an unfair name did for you and they really would understand.

Macques opened the window wider.

'No need to bring anything,' said Shorn.

This lot are very good, thought Macques as they helped him down from the window. Perhaps they're a high school drama group.

As he hurried across the front yard with them,

Macques had a thought. A quick flash of a thought that was stupid but he had it anyway because it felt so good even just for a fleeting moment.

How incredible and amazing and wonderful it would be if the Unfair Name Rescue Squad was real.

No.

Impossible.

Don't even hope.

Then Macques saw the lit-up sign on the roof of the taxi.

TACQUESI.

'Don't worry,' said Nickless, who was sitting next to Macques in the back of the taxi. 'This won't take long.'

'Only round the block,' said Jeen.

'Just as well these rescues are quick,' said Shorn from the front. 'We've got three more jobs tonight.'

Macques felt a stab of panic as they sped away down the dark street, partly because he'd always promised Mum and Dad he'd never get into a taxi with people he didn't know, and partly because Kaitye was driving and he was pretty sure she was too young to have a licence or third-party insurance.

At the top end of Macques's street they turned the corner.

'Where are you from?' asked Macques.

He wanted them to be real, he did so much, but part of his brain kept saying *TV show* and *I wonder where the camera's hidden.*

'The UNRS operates all over the world,' said Nickless. 'Thousands of us. And we're all flat out.'

'Dunno who kicked off this craze for dodgy names,' said Jeen. 'They should be locked up.'

The taxi turned another corner.

'Where are we going?' asked Macques.

'Home,' said Shorn.

'Your home,' said Kaitye.

Macques didn't understand.

'Your real home,' said Nickless.

Macques still didn't understand.

He was still trying to work out what they meant, and wondering if the TV show host was in the boot, when the taxi made the final turn of the block into the bottom end of Macques's street.

Macques knew it was his street because through the taxi window he could see the street sign, clear as anything in the light from a street lamp.

Knox Avenue.

Macques stared.

'Look,' he said. 'The spelling's changed. It's Knox, K-N-O-X.'

'That's right,' said Jeen.

Macques felt dizzy. Not in a horrible I'm-going-to-throw-up way. In a nice this-is-very-weird-but-I-don't-want-it-to-end way.

The taxi stopped outside Macques's house.

'That's it,' said Nickless. 'We're done. You're rescued.'

Nickless got out.

Macques realised he was meant to get out too, but he was finding it hard to actually move.

'Go,' said Shorn. 'We're on a schedule.'

Macques got out.

'How do I know this isn't all a dream?' he heard himself say to Nickless.

Nickless smiled and Macques had the feeling Nickless got asked that question a lot.

'How do you know all that stuff before we arrived wasn't a dream?' said Nickless.

Macques wished his thoughts weren't so scrambled.

He felt like one of those characters in a science fiction movie who gets taken at warp-speed into another dimension and arrives with bulging eyes and sticking-out hair and a smoking brain.

He put his hand to his head. His hair felt fine. But then he had only been round the block.

'Hope you like your parents,' said Nickless, getting back into the taxi and pulling the door shut.

Macques wasn't sure he'd heard that right. But it was too late to check. The taxi was driving away.

He gave the Unfair Name Rescue Squad a wave and watched the lit-up sign on the top of the taxi disappear into the darkness.

TAXI, it said.

Inside the house, everything looked exactly the same.

Well, almost. The wallpaper was a bit different, and the carpet, and there was a pine dresser in the hallway Macques didn't completely remember.

Macques stared at his reflection in the hall mirror.

His face looked the same and he felt wide awake.

There was nothing stuck to his back.

'Dinner's ready,' sang out Mum's voice.

Macques went into the living room. Mum and Dad were sitting at the table. They looked exactly the same too.

Well, almost.

They both looked slightly plumper and Mum's hair was curly instead of straight.

Macques started to feel a little bit panicked.

Then he saw something that made the panic go away. The big loving smiles on Mum and Dad's faces.

'Tuck in,' said Mum.

On the table were three plates of fish and chips. Mum was already stuffing quite a few chips into her mouth at once.

'Come on,' said Dad, winking at Macques. 'Make the most of it. You'll probably only be living at home for another ten years or so. Get Mum's cooking into you while you have the chance.'

Macques did just that. It was the best fish and chips he'd ever tasted. The more chips he put into his mouth, the happier he felt.

There were lots of questions buzzing around in his head, but they could wait till later.

Except one.

After a few more mouthfuls, Macques decided to get it over with.

'Mum and Dad,' he said. 'Can you test my spelling?'

Mum and Dad looked a bit nervous.

'OK,' said Dad. 'But we're pretty ordinary spellers.'

Macques couldn't help smiling to himself. Last time he'd asked Mum and Dad for a spelling test, they'd given him words like vicissitude and extracurricular and had gone on for hours about how important a big and impressive vocabulary was.

'You give me the word,' said Macques, 'and I'll spell it.'

'OK,' said Mum.

'Start with my name,' said Macques.

'You kind thing,' said Mum. 'Letting us all kick off with an easy one.'

'OK,' said Dad. 'Here goes.'

'Max,' said Mum.

'M-A-X,' said Macques.

He held his breath.

'Correct,' said Mum and Dad, grinning at him. 'Very good.'

Max grinned back.

They were right, it was very good.

As Mum leaned over and gave him a hug, Max took a peek at her socks.

Both grey.

They were ordinary and they matched.

Paparazzi

I crouch inside the front door, waiting for Kevin. I'm pretty nervous. That's why I'm chewing my nails. Yuk. This new nail polish looks good but it tastes revolting.

I've never done anything like this before. Usually on a Saturday afternoon I'm hanging out at Madonna's place or somewhere. But a friend needs me, that's why I've decided to do this. I just have to be careful I don't ruin everything by being seen.

There are paparazzi everywhere.

That's what Kevin reckons they're called. People who chase after you with cameras, desperate to get your picture, tripping over things, bumping into each other, invading your privacy, yelling at you to pull a funny face or sing something.

Why do families always do that?

Paparazzi sounds like an Italian word. I don't know what the *razzi* bit means, but I bet the *papa* part is because the person at the front with the biggest camera is usually your dad.

My mobile's ringing.

Two rings.

That's Kevin's signal. He must be almost here.

I open the front door and check for grown-ups. I hate to think what Mum and Dad would do if they saw me like this.

When I checked earlier, Dad was in the back yard trying out his new handicam. Mum was taking snaps of him on her digital 'cause she reckoned he looked so funny trying to video insects and walking into the washing.

From the sound of her giggles he must still have a bra on his head.

I hope they don't wake Daniel. Dan's not really into photos, but he'll always grab a couple with his mobile if there's a chance of getting his little sister into trouble.

The front yard is clear.

I pull the paper bag over my head and half walk half run down the front path.

Oh no, I haven't made the eye holes big enough.

I can't see anything either side of me.

My main worry is Mrs Kyneton next door. Her son got her a six megapixel 3G Nokia for Christmas and she's been putting the whole suburb on her blog ever since.

I don't think she's seen me.

I can't hear anyone yelling 'say cheese'.

What I can hear is Kevin's brother's car wheezing and spluttering as it gets closer.

I hope Kevin's right about the car being more mechanically reliable than it sounds.

It looks fantastic, a gleaming light-blue 1982 Valiant that always gets photographed at car shows, but looks aren't going to help us today.

The car squeaks to a stop. Kevin's in the front next to his brother. He winds down the window.

'Haul butt,' he says.

Even though I'm sweating with tension, I smile inside my paper bag. Kevin's got hair gel on. He thinks it makes him look like Brad Pitt. It does a bit, but his voice is even squeakier than the car.

'Hurry up,' says Kevin, starting to sound panicked.

I yank the back door open and scramble inside. The car roars away at high speed. That's what I wish it was doing. Actually it chugs away slowly.

'G'day Nat,' says Holly.

Holly is lying across the back seat, her head in a pillowcase. She squeezes over and I lie down next to her so nobody can see us from outside the car.

'Hi Natalie,' says Madonna.

Madonna is lying on the floor behind the front seats. She's got her head wrapped in a towel. It's her sister's sports towel from school. I can see the name tag. Beyonce Crutchley.

'Is it me,' says Madonna, 'or is it hot in here?'

'Sorry,' says Kevin's brother. 'Heater's jammed. I can't turn it off.'

'This isn't hot,' says Kevin. 'I had a go in a spin-dryer once and it was much hotter than this.'

None of us say anything.

Kevin is known all through grade six and most of grade five for exaggerating. It's what you have to do when you're the youngest of eight.

Suddenly the brakes slam on and I roll off the back seat onto Madonna.

'Ow,' she says.

'Sorry,' I say, and try to shift my bony bits.

'Does anyone know anybody with a yellow Corolla?' says Kevin's brother. 'It's blocking our way. There are people inside with cameras and they're waving at us. I think they want us to get out.'

My paper bag deflates. So does my chest.

It's my rellies. They must have come round the corner and seen me as I was getting into the car.

'It's my nan,' I say. 'And my auntie Pru and uncle Andrew. They've come over to take pictures of the Christmas clothes they gave me, but they're not meant to be here till this evening.'

'Paparazzi,' says Kevin. 'They don't care whose lives they wreck. I'll handle them.'

He gets out of the car.

'Kevin's amazing,' says his brother. 'He can lie his way out of anything. I've got videos of him doing it.'

Carefully I kneel up, not on Madonna, and peep out the window.

Kevin is yelling at Nan through the windscreen of the Corolla.

'It's an emergency,' he shouts. 'We've got to get to the hospital.'

Me and Holly look at each other through our paper bag and pillowcase eye holes.

Why is he telling them the truth?

In the Corolla, Nan looks puzzled too. She might not have her hearing aid turned up.

Auntie Pru winds down her window and points her camera at Kevin. It's the big one she uses for her wildlife photos on holiday. Kevin sees her and puts his hands up over his face and scurries back into our car.

'Don't worry, Kevin,' says Holly. 'You tried.'

'It's not my fault,' says Kevin indignantly. 'Look at the size of that zoom lens.'

None of us say anything, but we all know how he's feeling. We've all been caught by paparazzi not looking our best. We've all had our pimples and baggy track pants plastered across family slide nights and aunties' websites.

'They're backing up,' says Kevin's brother.

We chug off again.

I flatten myself onto the back seat, hoping they didn't hear what Kevin said about the hospital.

Why didn't he say we were going to the mall or somewhere?

It's not Kevin's fault. He must have panicked. I'd probably have done the same. Dealing with the paparazzi is just so stressful. I don't know how Angelina Jolie and that lot cope.

'Nat, keep your head down.'

Holly is hissing at me because I'm peeping out the car window.

I know she's right, but I can't help it. We're passing what's left of Tara's house and even though I've seen it heaps of times since the fire I can't stop myself looking.

Tara is the only kid in our class whose house has ever burned down.

A great big house turned into a pile of scrap and ash by a bunch of candles.

'Sheesh,' says Kevin's brother, slowing down and staring. 'I wouldn't mind getting a picture of that.'

'Not now,' pleads Kevin. 'We're on a deadline.'

'Yeah, yeah, I haven't forgotten,' says Kevin's brother. 'Keep your gel on.'

We don't stop.

I puff out my paper bag with relief.

But I don't blame Kevin's brother for wanting a picture. Each time I see the remains of Tara's burnt house I'm shocked because it's so much worse than I remember.

For example, I'd forgotten that the tiles in Tara's upstairs bathroom were pink. They're stacked up on the front lawn now, and most of them are singed and scorched and black round the edges.

Which is really sad because it was one of the nicest bathrooms I've ever been in.

But of course it's not as sad as what's happened to Tara.

'Poop.'

Kevin's brother is swearing.

The car's stalled and he can't get it started again. He pumps the pedal and the engine whines like a kid with pillow hair who doesn't want to be in a family photo.

'Are we out of gas?' says Kevin, who likes to use American words whenever possible.

'Battery's going flat,' says his brother. 'I need a push.'

'I'll handle it,' says Kevin and jumps out.

We don't even wait for him to try. Kevin's built like a TV aerial and even if he could move the car on his own he'd probably rupture one of his very skinny internal organs.

Plus we've got to be at the hospital in less than ten minutes.

'Keep your heads covered up,' Holly says to me and Madonna as we get out of the car.

She doesn't have to remind me. My paper bag is firmly on. To be sprung now would be a disaster.

We all push as hard as we can and the car starts moving.

'Hey,' yells a voice. 'Look. Kev's girlfriends have gone Islamic.'

I recognise the voice.

Rocco Fusilli.

I swivel my head and glare at him through my eyeholes. The one kid from school I hoped would be somewhere else today. Like Antarctica. But there he is, taunting us with his mates. They've got their mobiles out and as we break into a trot, pushing the car, they chase us and take pictures.

'Ignore them,' mutters Holly.

'You're invading our privacy,' Kevin yells at them. 'It's against the law. My dad's a cop and he's watching you on the police satellite.'

Rocco and his mates just laugh.

Kevin is always doing that, exaggerating about the surveillance capacity of the police.

Everyone knows that compared to rellies with cameras, most law enforcement agencies can't compete.

The car gives a big jolt and the engine splutters into life.

'Get in,' yells Holly.

We all clamber in and chug away from Rocco and his paparazzi pack.

I flop down in the back with Holly and Madonna. Inside my paper bag I'm sweating.

Just my luck.

I've got the most important photo session of my life coming up and I think my make-up's running.

We bump and totter into the hospital lift. Just the four of us because Kevin's brother has to stay with the car in case it gets scratched.

There are two nurses in the lift.

They stare at us.

I can feel Madonna shuffling nervously behind me and I know why. What if there's a hospital security regulation forbidding visitors to have their heads in bags or pillowcases? What if the nurses ring an alarm bell? What if security guards are waiting for us when the lift doors open and we don't even get to see Tara?

'Hi ladies,' says Kevin to the nurses, who glare at him sternly.

He's got courage, Kevin, for a skinny youngest kid in a big family.

'Don't be alarmed,' he says to the nurses. 'We're here to make a patient feel better.'

The nurses think about this, then both grin at him.

'Fair enough,' says one. 'They say laughter's the best medicine.'

'Which is why,' says the other, 'I predict a complete recovery when the patient sees your hair.'

The lift doors open and we drag Kevin out before he can get defensive about his gel.

As we hurry along the corridor I catch a glimpse of Tara's dad up ahead, going into Tara's ward.

I take a deep breath and keep going.

We knew Tara's rellies would be here for such an important occasion. The surprising thing is that her dad hasn't got his camera round his neck. Out of all our parents, he's the biggest photo fanatic. That's why Tara's house had so many burning candles in it, so their Christmas family pictures would look extra atmospheric.

On second thoughts, after what happened, he's probably gone right off photography.

We stop outside Tara's hospital room and peek cautiously in.

And nearly die.

It's not just Tara's rellies who are crowded around her bed. My mum and dad are there too. And Holly's. And Madonna's.

Kevin's aren't, but with eight kids they never are.

Mum and Dad and the others are staring at us.

None of them have got their cameras.

It's OK, I say to myself. Stay calm. We knew there was a chance this might happen. Everyone must have decided to keep cameras away from Tara.

I glance at Kevin. He pats his pocket.

'It's cool,' he says.

'G'day Nat,' says Mum uncertainly. 'Auntie Pru told us you were coming here and we guessed it must be Tara's special time so we thought we'd come and help cheer her up too. Why have you got a bag on your head?'

I don't say anything, partly because I'm a bit dizzy now the big moment is close and partly because a doctor is bending over Tara's bed, slowly unwinding the bandage from around her face.

We all stop looking at each other and anxiously watch the doctor and Tara.

It feels like nobody's breathing in the room, except Kevin who's looking a bit pale and like he might faint.

The last bit of bandage drops away from Tara's chin.

'Good,' says the doctor. 'That is good. It is. It's very good.'

Nobody else says anything.

It's as bad as we thought it would be.

The beautiful smooth skin on Tara's face isn't smooth any more and it hardly even looks like skin. It's bright red and cracked and flaky. And her hair, her long fair hair which was probably the most photographed hair outside Hollywood despite how Tara used to come up with some really clever hiding places to get away from her dad's camera, her hair isn't long any more.

It's short and very patchy.

You can see bits of her scalp.

'Give it a few weeks,' says the doctor to Tara. 'Few weeks and you'll be right as rain. Two months tops.'

Slowly, her hand shaking, Tara picks up the mirror on her bed and looks at herself.

I have a weird thought.

Can people whose faces have been burnt still cry?

They can. Tara's eyes are filling with tears as she looks at her reflection. I glance at Holly and Madonna through my eyeholes.

This is the moment.

I pull my paper bag off my head and Holly removes her pillowcase and Madonna unwraps her towel. We all stand there in front of Tara and let her see us.

I've prepared a speech about how she'll always be

our friend no matter what she looks like. But when I see the expression on her face as she stares at us through her tears I know I don't need to say anything.

I glance at Holly and Madonna.

I was right, our make-up has run, but I reckon we still look pretty good. Madonna's mum prefers orange lipstick, so Madonna's face isn't as red as Tara's, but Holly's is. And because we smeared the lipstick onto our faces really thickly and blasted it with our hairdryers, it's cracked and flaky and looks exactly like the real thing, specially on our foreheads.

I'm so glad we decided to give ourselves these short and patchy haircuts and shave our eyebrows off.

We look at Tara.

Tara looks at us.

Yes. It's working.

Tara isn't crying any more. She's even managing a smile.

'Thanks,' she whispers.

Mum and Dad and the other parents are staring at us like the doctor has just given them a really strong anaesthetic that knocks you out with your eyes open.

When it wears off there's a good chance they'll be

totally furious. Me and Holly and Madonna know this, but we think it's worth it.

The colour has come back into Kevin's face. Not as much as we've got, but at least he won't need oxygen.

I give him a nudge and he fumbles in his pocket. He pulls out his dad's camera and pushes it into Tara's dad's hands.

Then me and Holly and Madonna and Kevin go over and hug Tara and sit on the bed with our arms round her so the grown-ups, when they recover, can take our photo.

Good Dog

Veronica looks horrified when I arrive at her party.

She stands at the front door, her mouth open. The fluffy balls on her party dress wobble with alarm. The fake jewels on her tiara tremble with panic.

'Happy birthday,' I say.

She's not even looking at me, she's staring at Anthony.

'Woof,' says Anthony.

'A dog?' squeaks Veronica. 'Ginger, why did you bring a dog? My dad's not good with dogs.'

'I couldn't afford a present,' I explain. 'So I brought Anthony. You've been saying all week you hope your party will be a success. Well Anthony's here to help. He's a party dog.'

Veronica gives a little whimper.

'Don't worry,' I say. 'I know Anthony's big, but he's friendly. He won't hurt your dog.'

Veronica glances nervously over my shoulder.

'Our dog isn't here,' she says. 'My dad's in the park, training it.'

She doesn't have to tell me. I can hear Mr Pobjoy's angry voice drifting over from the park across the road.

'Bad dog,' he's yelling. 'Bad dog.'

I swap a look with Anthony.

Mr Pobjoy should be in the army. We live two streets away and most evenings I can hear him roaring at that poor dog even over the noise of Mum and Dad's music in the kitchen.

Anthony hates hearing another dog being treated like that. Usually he sticks his head under one of our cats so he doesn't have to listen to it.

Now he just wants to get inside.

'Stop,' says Veronica to Anthony. 'Come back.'

Anthony has squeezed past her into the house.

'Party dogs hate having to wait outside,' I explain. 'They want to get in and start partying.'

We hurry inside after Anthony.

The party is in the family room. About ten kids are on leather chairs in front of a huge TV. The boys are fighting and the girls are complaining and they're all throwing party food at each other.

'Good grief,' says Veronica's mum when she sees Anthony. 'That's all I need.'

Mrs Pobjoy is very stressed. Her fashionable clothes have got quite a lot of marshmallow dip on them. Her very fashionable hair, which Mum reckons would cost more to have done than some countries spend on food, is looking a bit sweat-affected.

'Is that your dog?' Mrs Pobjoy says to me.

'Yes,' I say. 'His name's Anthony. I'm Ginger. I sit next to Veronica in class.'

I hold out my hand to shake Mrs Pobjoy's. She doesn't see it.

'Pets were not invited,' she says to Veronica.

'I didn't invite it,' says Veronica miserably. 'She just arrived with it.'

'It's OK,' I say to Mrs Pobjoy. 'Anthony's here to help.'

Mrs Pobjoy still looks stressed.

I explain to her how Anthony was already a party

expert when I got him. How when I first saw him in the pound he was playing What's The Time Mr Wolf? with all the other dogs. Letting them creep up behind him, then turning and chasing them till they nearly wet themselves with excitement.

'That is the stupidest thing I've ever heard,' says Mrs Pobjoy crossly.

'It's not,' I say. 'Anthony's a mixture of wolfhound and English sheepdog. Wolfhounds are very fun-loving and English sheepdogs have to organise a lot of party games out in the fields to keep the sheep warm in winter.'

'Get it out of here,' says Mrs Pobjoy.

'Look,' says Veronica, pointing.

Anthony is already rounding up the kids for the first game, nudging and nuzzling them off the couch. When someone doesn't want to move, Anthony grabs a corner of their party frock or best shirt between his teeth and gently drags them.

Some of the kids are screaming and trying to run away. Others are trying to hide under the chairs. This always happens when Anthony arrives at a party. Kids get over-excited.

'The first game's Hide And Seek,' I say to the screamers and runners. 'It's fun. Do what the others are doing. Hide somewhere you don't think Anthony will find you.'

Kids hurl themselves into cupboards and clamber up onto shelves.

Soon everyone is hidden. Except for Mrs Pobjoy, who is outside in the barbecue area, glowering at Anthony and talking very fast into her mobile.

Anthony starts finding everyone.

Some people are so worked up they almost faint when Anthony sticks his big head into the laundry basket or nest of tables they're hiding in. He does have very big teeth, which can be a bit of a problem for a party organiser.

But when he licks your face, which is his way of saying *good hiding place, but I found you*, you know he wouldn't hurt a fly. Not even an over-excited fly who's had way too many lollies.

By the end of the game, some kids are grinning. Even Veronica isn't looking so upset, probably because she won by hiding in her dad's wine cellar.

'Good on you,' I whisper to Anthony.

He made sure he found Veronica last. That's the

advantage of being a mixture of breeds. You get to be not only clever, but also kind on birthdays.

'What's next?' someone yells.

Anthony is already organising the next game, wagging his big tail and herding everybody into a line.

'Musical Chairs,' I say, grabbing the dining chairs and putting them into a line too.

Anthony starts singing. Well, howling really. He can sort of do some of Mum and Dad's Rod Stewart tunes. Well, bits of them.

A few of the kids look like they want to go back to playing Hide And Seek.

I know why. When Anthony sings, he does spray quite a lot of saliva around. It's the one other problem he has as a party organiser.

But his timing's great. He waits for me to whisk another chair away, then stops howling at really unexpected moments. Each time he does, kids are laughing and falling over each other to get their bums on a seat.

Veronica is laughing too. She can see her party's going really well.

Then a loud voice booms out.

'Whoa. What's going on here?'

The room goes quiet. We all turn and see a man in a business suit standing in the doorway. He's got a mobile phone in one hand and a very small white dog in the other.

'It's OK, Dad,' pleads Veronica. 'We're having a really good time. Anthony's a really good party org . . .'

Her voice trails off. Mr Pobjoy is glaring at her.

'Bad girl,' he says.

Veronica tries to shrink inside her party dress.

Mr Pobjoy points at Anthony.

'What are you thinking, Veronica,' he says, 'bringing a brute like that in here? It could tear Flossy Evangeline Diamante to pieces. Good grief, you know how much we paid for Flossy.'

Veronica is close to tears.

'Two thousand dollars,' she says in a tiny voice.

The rest of us stare at the little white dog in amazement. That must work out at more than a thousand dollars a kilo. Even Anthony is looking stunned.

'Poor little Flossy,' says Mr Pobjoy. 'Look at her. She's trembling. She's terrified.'

No she's not. She's curled up contentedly and

looking down at Anthony with keen interest. Veronica's the one who's trembling and upset.

Suddenly Flossy jumps down from Mr Pobjoy's hand, trots over to Anthony and starts sniffing his bottom. Well, sniffing his legs, because there's no way she can reach his bottom without a small ladder.

'Flossy,' snaps Mr Pobjoy. 'Come back here.'

Flossy ignores him.

'Bad dog,' he yells at her. 'Bad dog.'

Flossy still ignores him.

Anthony gives her a sniff because that's the polite thing to do. And also, I can tell, because he feels a bit protective. She's a small dog being yelled at by a big man.

'Bad dog,' roars Mr Pobjoy again.

Anthony tilts his head down next to Flossy's and gently licks her ear a few times. It's almost like he's whispering to her.

Suddenly Flossy trots back over to Mr Pobjoy, who gives an angry but satisfied nod.

Flossy stops right next to his feet and pees on his shoes.

'Bad dog,' yells Mr Pobjoy, jumping back and trying

to shake the pee off his feet, his voice going squeaky with outrage.

The rest of us are trying not to laugh. Several of the kids aren't managing it very well. I see Anthony looking at me with his big brown eyes and something in his expression gives me an idea. I speak up before Veronica's dad sends us all home.

'Mr Pobjoy,' I say. 'I'm quite experienced with dogs and I know how hard it can be to train them. One thing that's worked really well for me is a party game called Good Dog Bad Dog.'

Mr Pobjoy looks at me long and hard.

I can see that what he really wants to do is chuck us all out so he can yell at Flossy and Veronica in private. But he's been trying to train Flossy for weeks. Underneath his expensive suit and his hair transplant, I'm guessing he's desperate.

'Please, Dad,' says Veronica. 'Give it a go.'

'Good Dog Bad Dog?' mutters Mr Pobjoy, not sounding convinced.

Mrs Pobjoy has been off and changed her clothes and she's looking a bit less stressed.

'You might as well give it a go, Vince,' she says

wearily to her husband. 'You've said yourself Flossy is a difficult dog.'

Mr Pobjoy frowns suspiciously.

'How does this game work?' he says.

'It's simple,' I say. 'For the next five minutes, all we're allowed to say is either *good dog* or *bad dog*.'

Mr Pobjoy looks doubtful.

Please, I urge him silently. Give it a go.

My plan is dead simple. To show Mr Pobjoy that kindness gets better results than yelling. Though you'd think a top business manager like him would already know that.

'OK,' I say. 'Let's start.'

I look at Anthony to make sure he understands what we're doing. I can tell from the way he looks at me that he does.

I'm going to say *good dog* to him lots of times and he's going to do lots of clever tricks and obedient things to show Mr Pobjoy that *good dog* always works better than *bad dog*.

Flossy is sniffing Anthony's leg again. Anthony starts licking Flossy's ear again in a murmuring sort of way.

Before I can get my first *good dog* out, Mr Pobjoy, whose shoes are still wet, turns to Anthony.

'Bad dog,' he snaps.

Anthony looks at him for a moment, then does something that isn't really what you'd expect from a good dog.

He leans forward, opens his huge jaws, places them around Flossy, and closes them.

Flossy disappears.

Inside Anthony's mouth.

Veronica screams.

So do the other kids.

Mrs Pobjoy clutches the pool table.

I feel faint. I can hear the distant echo of something a dog-hater once said to me. That you can never trust pound dogs. That sooner or later they always turn vicious.

Then I see Anthony is looking at me. He isn't chewing or swallowing, just looking at me patiently. The bulge in his mouth is still moving.

Suddenly I know what he's doing.

He isn't turning vicious, he's just playing Good Dog Bad Dog his way.

'No,' howls Mr Pobjoy. 'Flossy. That brute has eaten Flossy.'

I turn to Veronica, whose fluffy party-dress balls are trembling almost as much as her lips.

'Rescue Flossy,' I whisper to Veronica. 'You won't get hurt, I promise. Just say *good dog*.'

Veronica stares at me.

I can see this isn't the birthday party she was hoping for.

'Better hurry,' I whisper. 'Flossy's running out of air in there.'

Veronica goes nervously over to Anthony. She has to step around her father, who is yelling insulting things at Anthony again.

'Bad dog,' he's shouting. 'Bad dog. Bad dog.'

Anthony ignores him and turns to face Veronica, his jaws still closed.

I can just make out faint tremors of movement inside his mouth.

Veronica hesitates. Then I see Anthony looking into her eyes and I know everything's going to be OK.

Veronica can hardly get the words out.

But she does.

'Good dog,' she whispers to Anthony.

'Mr Pobjoy,' I say. 'Look. Veronica's saving Flossy.'

And she is.

'Good dog,' she says, and Anthony slowly opens his mouth. Veronica puts her hands inside and lifts out a soggy, bedraggled, stunned-looking Flossy.

'Woof,' says Flossy.

'Good dog,' says Veronica.

'Thank God,' says Mr Pobjoy, taking Flossy from Veronica. 'Flossy, sweetie. It's OK, you're safe. Good dog. Good dog.'

He hugs Flossy.

'Good dog,' he says, over and over.

Then he hugs Veronica.

'Good girl,' he says to her. 'Good girl.'

Veronica is tearful again, but in a way that lets us all see this is the best party she's ever had.

'Good on you,' I whisper to Anthony.

Mr Pobjoy stops hugging Flossy and Veronica, and looks over at me and Anthony.

'I think it's best,' he says tersely, 'if you both leave.'

Then he goes back to hugging his dog and his daughter.

I don't argue.

On the way out, Veronica's mum catches up with us.

'Thank you,' she says. 'Thank you both so much. Veronica's cousin is having a party next week. I don't suppose you and Anthony can come?'

'That's very kind,' I say. 'I think we can.'

I check with Anthony.

He licks my hand.

I can see he likes the idea of another party.

We both do.

About the author

Morris Gleitzman grew up in England and came to Australia when he was sixteen. He was a frozen-chicken thawer, sugar-mill rolling-stock unhooker, fashion-industry trainee, student, department-store Santa, TV producer, newspaper columnist and screen-writer. Then twenty-five years ago he had a wonderful experience. He wrote a novel for young people. Since then he's been one of Australia's most popular children's authors.

Visit Morris at his website:

morrisgleitzman.com